A CONTRADICTION
OF SANDPIPERS

Martin Jones

To Rachael

best wishes

Martin

A CONTRADICTION
OF SANDPIPERS

CHAPTER 1

A smart gentleman suggested I attend the Ragged School in the Strand. I thanked him before confirming that I prefer to entrust my education to a patterer. You might not know what a patterer is, but I am confident you have met one in your own line. Every business has them, offering beguiling talk as a kind of merchandise in itself, to buyers who thus do not expect an exact equivalent for their money. A younger son cut out of inheritance, an educated man enjoying his drink too much, a churchman lapsed of faith, or maybe a fine needlewoman, once in Paris, now embroidering French verbal flourishes in the selling of her fashions from a street barrow. They all come to us, and become patterers. For a few years now Mr Almanac had been directing my education, in return for some of the money I made part-time as a sewer tosher, supplemented by our pearly king, Rawbone, who grouped me with his vulnerables requiring charity.

Almanac was a type of patterer we call a flying stationer, roving from pitch to pitch, the excitement moving with him. I present him here in action.

"Come now all you good gentlemen, ladies, young, old and otherwise."

He'd go upwards and particular loud on the *wise* in 'other*wise*' which always got a laugh, everyone looking at each other and wondering who was otherwise.

"I have wonders for your delectation today. We have accounts - eyewitness mind you - of a duel between the Countess of Devonshire and Lady Charlotte Adams-Smyth, following welching on a debt of gambling. And not only are my witnesses good with their eyes they are good with pen and *ink*."

Almanac, going large on the word *ink*, had his listeners riding up over a humpback bridge as they came along with him.

"We have new stories of mendacious robberies, impossible murders in the best of houses, and the kind of delusive suicides, where if only the young man had hung on one more short hour, the object of his affections would have been his. So make a queue in a good British manner and partake of the kind of literature that will take you to Heaven and *Hell*, and bring you back in time for a glass of stout at the Red *Lion*! And that means you as well, Master John."

Picked out of the crowd in a contingent way, this old fella, Master John, received a hug from nearby ladies, as if he had personally been to Heaven and Hell on military campaign, and was enjoying a welcome back.

This above description applied when Mr Almanac was a fit man. Now he was not so well, his skin giving the appearance of pages in a book stored too long in a damp attic. These days, he got by solely with his tutoring of people like me. I resided at his Rosemary Lane chambers, located over a bakery. There was a capacious study, with two rooms on each side devoted to children and what seemed to be two wives, maybe one for each half of the accommodation. I didn't enquire very closely. Upstairs in the attic, there were another couple of rooms where us students lodged.

Almanac took me out onto what he called his loggia, which was the flat bakery roof, upon which, with some shoddy walls and wishful thinking, he had created a balcony reaching out from the book-lined study. If you craned your neck and screwed up your eyes and used your imagination, our eyrie offered an expansive view of the river. He always tried to come out here, even if it was too early in the year for comfort. The only saving grace was a shimmer of tepid bakery emanations through the floor.

We came to a topic that had been hanging over me for months now, the question of what I would do with my literary education.

"I feel I have now decided on the character of writing I wish to pursue."

"Excellent. About time."

A shaft of chilly evening sunshine reached us through a tumble of roofs, providing the sort of heat only serving to warm one side of you, leaving the other side colder. Almanac sat down at our balcony table, shouting a request in the direction of the book-lined, vaporous dimness of his interior.

"Flora, bring me a porter, won't you?"

Flora bustled out, slamming down on the table a dark bottle lacking the manners of a label. Almanac thought better of asking for a tankard. He got up and found that himself, before slopping a generous measure of boot-polish-brown liquid into a bewhiskered mouth.

"Would you like to partake?"

"I will respectfully decline."

"Suit yourself. You were about to tell me your direction. Is it to be the writing of political tracts, as I suggested? Have you reflected on the evils of society and the importance of an author in revealing them?"

"I have tried to reflect, but the evils of society seem distant for me."

"No political writings then, Tim?"

My silence confirmed that this was not to be my course.

"No? Well, it is true that you have a good life, a naturally sunny disposition and a lack of politics. It seems unlikely we will get any tracts for the changing of society out of you.

Entertainment then? Just now there is a market for fictitious love letters of Italian noblemen."

"I don't know if fictitious letters are the right course either."

There was a growing rapidity to Almanac's breathing. A sweaty pallor appeared to be draining away the life from his face. The signs were obvious, looking back.

"What about..." Almanac took a long drag of porter. "What about the writing of puff to sell patent medicines?"

"What I wish to do is write songs. I have not told you this before, but I have been working with some musicians at the Wilton."

"Songs? Comic or ballad?"

"Neither. My associates are called Belle and Whistle, sir. They're skilful and of an original cast of mind."

"A duet? A duet is more likely to work if it's a comic turn."

"We don't want to do comic material. The fact of the matter is we are trying music with kroomen rhythm. And we have a third person now, Long Tom - you know him from the pearly parades. He plays drums."

As I was saying this, it struck me that all dreams sound unlikely when you describe them aloud. You open your mouth, out pour ridiculous words, and in pours the magic-draining lights of day, leaving your nighttime carnival a sad littered field. But if your dream is to become something for the full twenty four hours, it has to withstand the dawn.

"Kroomen music?"

"You know, the music of African coves who sing at the docks."

"African coves who sing at the docks?" Almanac made a third visit to his porter "Are you joking with me, boy? You must be. If you cannot decide on something sensible, I will be forced to do so on your behalf. You are a competent writer and have reached the stage now where you can be of help to me. Instead of wasting your talent, and all the effort we have put into you, it's time to go to work. I need assistance with some research."

"Mr Almanac...."

"I am told by my contacts that there is a story brewing with regard to the royal family; some kind of scandal involving cards. The royals always sell well. I want you to go and talk to a man named Forbes; find out what's going on. Start earning some money, to pay Rawbone back for all the faith he has shown in you."

"The Royal Family?"

I did not wish to appear rude, but it was hard to cover the sound of air parping out from my unrealised ambitions.

"Yes, the royals. A royal story is always popular. I'm only trying to do my best for someone who thinks he can make a living writing verse to the rhythm of African music."

"I don't want to sound ungrateful; and it's the truth that I appreciate all you and Rawbone have done for me. But the royals? I don't know anything about them."

"Find out then, lad. And what you can't find out, make up."

"You said books were good for us, helping us see more widely. You said they were truthful. I'm not sure if what you're suggesting meets that mould."

Almanac's tankard, which had been wavering in the whiskery vicinity of black and purple lips, now slammed down on the table.

"You vile youth. Who in damnation do you think you are!"

Almanac leapt to his feet, eyes glistering and spittle flying. I had seen this before, and noted it as the probable reason Almanac was no longer teaching at an Oxford college, which was his due. He sometimes had episodes, and due to my cussedness, he was having one now. These involved destroying anything in sight. The fact that there was not much on Almanac's balcony to destroy only added to his frustration. The chairs gave some satisfaction, held by their legs and brought down upon the table. This had an added benefit of also demolishing the table, in stages, one chair at a time. After the furniture had been reduced to a jumble of firewood, there wasn't much left to focus ire upon, since Almanac's lashing-out mercifully did not involve people, except as the accidental result of flying debris. With the look of a man suffering thirst visions in the desert, heading for an oasis that does not exist, he made his way through the open balcony doors in the direction of his books, burgundy and brown on their shelves.

"No, not the books," I implored.

Flora rushed in with a raised rolling pin.

Almanac had his hands claw-like across a row of volumes, which he would never be able to replace. Each one cost an average weekly wage. They were an echo of a former life he would not live again.

"Not the books, Mr Almanac."

This appeal seemed to return the man to his senses. Enervated fingers slipped from vellum bindings. He glanced up, and then dropped his head, suggesting both exhaustion and humility. Flora lowered the rolling pin. It was impossible to sit down due to a lack of serviceable chairs, so Almanac leant against his books, now serving to provide physical as well as moral support.

"I see in you the youngster I once used to be. I was equally annoying. Maybe you will have better luck. But until then, I'll get in touch with Forbes, a patterer like myself, who talked himself into a job as footman at the palace. Find out about this royal story."

CHAPTER 2

Almanac had told me to go to The Grapes in Limehouse. Getting there was easier than I thought it would be, on account of running into Rawbone. Rawbone is a one-time sailor, tosher, finder, adventurer and now occasional waterman. Most of the energy he has left, which is considerable for a man advanced in years, goes to his charitable pearly activities. He is a great man, as shining as those pearls lining the seams of his black waistcoat.

I was flotsam on Wapping Street, crossing the footway at Wapping Basin, when a distant seaman's ahoy reached me across the river. Aboard a small boat out on grey water, I could make out tiny gesticulations. A few minutes later, on a scrappy patch of beach near Wapping Steps, Rawbone's bow scraped into gravel. I jumped aboard, pushing us off with the landward leg. After three heavy pulls, blades sucking deep, there I was, King Neptune, plucked from obscurity to reign mighty on the Thames.

Regarding Rawbone at his oars, any such grandiose feelings slipped away. Rawbone thinks a lot of me, which is humbling. It makes me want to do right by him, seeing as he has provided pearly money for my education. I resolved to put the song writing in second place and see through my new writing job, as Almanac had asked of me.

"Where are you bound, young Tim?"

"The Grapes," I said to the waterman's hard working back. "Almanac says I am to meet Forbes there and get details of some royal shillyshally. He thinks there's a scandal sheet in it, which should pay well."

"I don't know if that's right for you, Tim," said Rawbone half turning to offer this opinion over his shoulder.

"Almanac says it's proper work, the sort of thing I need to do to pay you all back."

"Maybe," replied Rawbone, looking off to the Bermondsey side where some invisible advice seemed to be blowing in the wind.

It was with a cheery wave that Rawbone dropped me off on the foreshore beneath The Grapes, saying he would be back for me in an hour. I took this kindness as a reminder of where my duty lay. Giving him a firm shove-off felt like too little service. Song writing was for dreams. Writing scandal sheet stories about royalty was for making a living and paying back those who had been good to me.

There, standing upon pebbles slimy from recent tide, I looked up at a construction that might have been a public house, or the stern of a tiny man o' war, somehow caught between north bank warehouses. Built upon the embankment's mouldering piles, she was a two decker, with the top tier overhanging. Each deck had three latticed windows, those of the lower deck offset from those above, to make allowance for a door tucked away, port side. This whole structure presented an uneven, curving, maritime quality. I now began to climb a vertical ladder, up towards the lower deck. Above me, an old sea dog in the outfit of a captain's steward, leant against an uneven rail as if staring out over the Barbary Coast, rather than Rotherhithe. His eyes followed me up the ladder, narrowed as if against a tropic sun.

"What have we picked up 'ere then?"

"I'm looking for Forbes."

"He ain't around, but there's someone else as wants to see

you. He asked me to stand look out. We serve on the same ship."

"A ship? But I thought Forbes worked at Buckingham Palace."

The old sailor cackled deep down in his chest, which sounded like Davy Jones's locker pulled ashore, still half full of water after long immersion.

"The palace is like a big ship. Lots of my sort work there. We are suited you might say. Anyhow, you go in."

I pushed through the door into a subdued saloon. Once inside, it was almost possible to discern an ocean-going creak of timbers moving about me. My spirits dropped when I saw who was sitting in the best place next to the fire, warming himself like butter upon bacon this raw day.

"Look who it is," said Boggo Weedy, sitting back in his chair like a lord. Everyone else in the saloon sat forward on elbows, tables taking their weight, as though weary with the climbing of rigging topside. "This is the young man who wants to be our new Mr Dickens."

"I don't want to be Mr Dickens."

"You could do worse, my lad. Is he alone?" asked Boggo of the lookout.

"Old Rawbone brought him in, but he's rowed off now."

Boggo turned his attention back to me, waving a handkerchief, which I realised was a signal that I could sit opposite him.

"Where's Forbes?"

"Never mind about him. I have found out about your literary ambitions and would like to help."

"But Almanac said I was to meet Forbes."

"He's otherwise engaged. I have told him that the job of giving you advice today falls to me. Now, boy, I think the Board of Works could use a young man like you, who, from what I hear, is excellent with a pen. I also know you have no parents now, and owe Rawbone a sum of pearly money, which means there's a pressing need to support yourself."

While Boggo was not a man of easy company, it would be unwise to cross him. I tried to look confident, without appearing so full of myself that I might land a smart one on his smirky mouth.

"How is it going as Her Majesty's Rat and Mole Destroyer, Mr Weedy?"

I tried to make my question sound as though I was envious of the life that Boggo must be leading.

"The responsibility is heavy, boy. Rats threaten the fabric of Buckingham Palace; and as for moles, those are the evil creatures who took the life of our great sovereign, King William. The treacherous mounds thrown up by those beasts in Richmond Park tipped the mount of a British monarch into a fatal stumble. It is my job to make sure that such a thing never happens again."

It was as though moles served as foreign assassins, trained by the French to dig tunnels under the Channel, from whence they emerged to threaten the British state.

"So yes, in answer to your question, my life as Rat and Mole Destroyer to Her Majesty has profound responsibilities, which I take seriously. That is what the clever class of people are here for, boy - people like us. It is our job to shoulder burdens on behalf of our fellow man, to make our country a better place, a brighter beacon for the world. You know that there was a time when I lived amongst you. I have never forgotten from whence I came, and my responsibility to help those I have left behind. Like yourself, Tim, I was a protégé of Almanac. Did you know that?"

"I did not, sir."

My answer was truthful. Almanac had never mentioned Boggo.

"People like us must help those who are not as clever and able. That is why I would like you to come with me to the Board of Works. What I propose is this. Write some tracts about your... shall I call it, life...?"

The old lookout man, now propping the bar, laughed a watery laugh at Boggo's supposed joke. In answering, I made an effort to keep resentment out of my voice.

"I was given reason to believe you were to talk to me about some problem regarding Prince Edward and a game of baccarat?"

"You are to forget all that kind of tittle tattle, right now. For shame, boy. You are better than some scandal sheet. Don't you think so?"

Boggo had trussed me up, like a lawyer who can inflict, or wash away, guilt with a few clever words to the bench.

"Write about your life as a sewer tosher. Hold nothing back, mind. Fear not for the sensibilities of those in fine houses who might swoon at the verisimilitude of your depiction. We have to be truthful, no matter what the consequences to ladies who hold gloved hands to elegant mouths and noses, gagging against the stink that you paint with your words. Describe sudden, treacherous floods roaring down a tunnel faster than a man can run, or rats surrounding a lone man, so when later his body is found, nothing but picked bones remain. Use your talent to describe subhuman work that takes you and your kind far from God's light, scrabbling for scraps in city sewers, like the very vermin living down there."

Boggo looked at me waiting for my reaction, which I suppose he thought would be enthusiastic agreement that the life of a sewer tosher was not to be recommended. But if he wanted truthfulness, then verily I enjoyed toshing. Strictly speaking, he was right about hazardous floods. But what was this nonsense about rats overwhelming lone men? How did a rat catcher believe such stuff? Rats aren't bad creatures. They are like people in many ways, enjoying their routine, loving their food, and having no qualms about where they get it. People are the same, though they dress things up with silver cutlery and linen napkins.

Boggo waited for me to join him in his crusade. A single top button holding his jacket around his shoulders like a cloak, strained against his enthusiasm.

"That's a bit strong, Mr Weedy," was all I could finally say. After all, Boggo had, without so much as dancing around the subject, referred to me and my friends as rats, which were equal with moles in his league of lowest creatures in the world.

"Tell it as it is," declared Boggo, rearing up like a strutting cock in a farmyard which he assumes is the entire universe. "You must help show the truth, so the Board of Works can get toshers out of the sewers. Then we can start on the costers - shepherd them into regulated markets. Street people are an embarrassment, a danger to themselves and others."

This was too much. A man as powerful as Boggo should not be crossed, but such abuse was insupportable. I opened my mouth to tell him what he could do with his good intentions, only to be interrupted by a disturbance out on deck. The lookout attended the river door, where a visitor now stood in an urgent kind of way. In response to the visitor's rapid but muffled words, there was nodding, stroking of beards and placing of thumbs inside braces where they sat over shirts. Judging the situation to be of sufficient importance for our meeting to be interrupted, Mr Lookout directed the visitor over to us.

"Message from the palace, your..."

For one awful moment, I thought this skulking new arrival was going to call Boggo, 'Your Grace' or something similar. Fortunately, he refrained at the last moment.

"Message from the palace, sir. There's been an item lost."

"What sort of item?"

"A ring. The Queen's ring, which she received from the

Prince Consort himself."

"My God!"

"There's more. Her Majesty thinks she might have last seen the ring in the…"

"Come on, man, where did she lose it? Spit it out."

The messenger lowered his voice, as though the location he wanted to mention and the person of Her Majesty could not with any degree of decorum be put together.

"It seems she may have lost the ring in the privy closet, sir, of the private quarters."

"The closet? The close closet? Good God almighty in all his mercy. Do you know what this means?"

"I do, sir, though the Queen will not have it said."

"Of course not. It is not for her to worry about where it might have gone. That's for us to do for her. We must get back to the palace."

"I will call your carriage around to the front."

"Never mind about that. Get a waterman to row me back. It will be quicker to Westminster by boat. Look lively."

I was forgotten as Boggo roared to his feet, his jacket flapping around that struggling top button. Pushing the messenger ahead of him, he made for the river deck, his disappearance leaving an echo of door banging.

That was the end of my interview.

"He's gone then," said Alfred the one legged barman, stating the obvious.

"It seems he had pressing business, what with being so responsible."

"All them moles and rats won't catch themselves. Stay away from him, Tim. Use your talents to read newspapers to the likes of us who can't read. We need you to writ our letters. You don't want to go down no road he's gone down."

"I wasn't expecting to see him, Alf. I thought it was going to be someone else."

"Boggo always sticks his oar in. Anyways, until Rawbone comes back for you, can you help me with this?"

Alfred held up a copy of a newspaper, which by the look of it had not been presented to him ironed on a silver tray.

"That's *The Examiner*, Alfred," I started to say, aiming to continue with advice to try something a little less high. But I sensed people listening. It was not my job to embarrass a good man in his place of work.

"Find an article, Alf, and we'll take a look at it."

"And while we're about it, young Hancock over there needs help with writing some particulars for the Navy."

"What particulars?"

"Particulars saying he can write."

"But he can't write, Alf."

"The Navy don't really care about that. They just need him to say he does. Not much writing gets done on ships now, does it?"

"That's certainly true."

Why anyone would want to be in the Navy is to me a mystery, but I helped Hancock, and Alf, and was busy reading an article by John Stewart Mill to a group of stevedores when Rawbone walked in.

Out on the river heading back to Blue Anchor Yard, I knew Rawbone was not happy.

"Well I 'ope you feel that was an honest day's work," he said pulling at his oars. I was sitting in the stern this time, so we could converse on a more proper face to face basis.

"It was a waste of time, Rawbone. Forbes wasn't there. It was Boggo Weedy. He wanted me to go to the Board of Works and write about how terrible our life is as toshers."

Rawbone's reply had a colour to it.

"You mustn't give no help with that. Boggo thinks he can advance hisself at the Board of Works by pushing to make toshing illegal, because it's For Our Own Good. It's also for Boggo's own good, because his nasty campaign makes him look progressive to his fancy Works friends, sipping champagne at their clubhouse in Spring Gardens."

We sculled on for a while, getting towards Blue Anchor pier.

"And why did he rush off in such a hurry?" asked Rawbone. But he was not able to listen to my answer right then, because by now we were gliding through a noisy mangrove of masts, black hulls, smoke stacks and hanging rigging.

"A little right, Rawbone," I cautioned as a barge began to push off in front of us. The quay was a game of netted loads and sack-burdened barrows leaning their crushing weight against men dragging and balancing at that nice place where it's not heavy at all. How everything moved so amongst that maze of crates and sacks was a mystery to me, bamboozling the brain just as much as one of those tangled trick knots that somehow drops out once you pull two ends.

Rawbone drifted into a squeeze, the boat knocking against the quay. We tied up, and took us a step that pushed down into the boat followed by a step where the ground pushed up into our feet. Rawbone touched his cap in reply to similar marks of respect coming from those with their hands free.

Now it was the noise that prevented me answering Rawbone's question about Boggo's rapid departure. To fill this pause, I will tell you about the racket. There were clanking chains whirling on steam driven wheels - like a whole beach of pebbles tumbling down a shoot - men's shouts, a huff huff of hard-breathing steam engines, and a top line of crying seagulls, who seemed thrilled by the whole business. Retreating in the distance were booming horns, where the pitch told you how big the vessel that owned it would be. Very deep, right away over warehouses and bridges, out beyond the great river expanse, rendering distant buildings tiny against a grey sky - that's where the biggest ships wallowed in the sonorousness of their abyssal horns. Right out there was the kind of sound that comes from many noises all blending into a kind of universal roar. Against all this vast clamour, near and far, Rawbone's conversational voice brought me back from the ends of the Earth.

"So, tell me; why was Boggo riding down the river, driving on his waterman like a horse over Aintree's last furlong?"

"Oh that was some bobbins about the Queen's lost ring," I replied, casual in my possession of royal news, even of the insignificant variety. We were walking on the outskirts of the port crush now, Rawbone casting questions to me, head down, his cap shading his eyes and the conversation.

"Where did she lose it?"

"In the right royal privy closet it seems, Rawbone."

"In the what? Don't you realise what this means? I thought you was supposed to be the clever one. If she lost a ring in the closet, that means it must have jumped itself off her royal finger straight down the plug hole into our neck of the woods. Wait 'til Old Ma hears about this."

CHAPTER 3

Why should this desire to write have grabbed hold of me? Does a similar vocation land upon the shoulders of draughtsmen who draw in chalk upon the pavement, or those who cut profiles in black paper? All I know is that the pull to it, in those with susceptibility, is strong. I have known writers without hands on the streets of this city, and if that doesn't demonstrate something, I don't know what will.

When it does grab hold of you, the pull goes in two directions - one path aspires to dreams, the other to reality. Reality was meeting with a Buckingham Palace patterer, to discover his scummy royal news, or Boggo wanting my help dragging the reputation of toshers through the mud. The dream, meantime, was writing songs. After leaving the docks, this ambition required me to loop around on myself, heading back to Wapping, this time to find Belle and Whistle at the Wilton. There was still a portion of guilt, which said I should be pursuing sensible money-making writing, a feeling sharpened by the recent kindness of Rawbone.

You come up to the Wilton along Grace's Alley, a narrow passage that makes me think of a quay, with anchored ships jostling in, stern first, on both sides. Along the cobbles, there is room for a hansom cab and not much else. Any pedestrian like myself, has to be ready for leaping and pressing against a wall in a desperate bid to save his life from casual highway death. Such were the risks I accepted to undertake my calling.

Unscathed, I reached the Prince of Denmark public house, which serves as a kind of antechamber to the Wilton.

"This above all, to thine own self be true."

These words I muttered, entering into the Denmark's Mahogany Bar. Beyond was the deeper fastness of the Wilton Music Hall, glorious behind the pub. But I was not actually to reach that hall, because the pub cellar was my destination today.

"Morning, Vince."

As far as Vince is concerned anything until early evening counts as morning, given his employment hours.

"That letter I wrote for you to the excise, did it hit the mark?"

"You're a good lad, Tim. You go right down."

So it was into the cellar I made my way, sounds of argument coming up to meet me.

Down here, my act Belle and Whistle, the duo that did not want to be a comic act, were supposed to be at work upon their music. It was, however, a comic scene of discord that I found. Long Tom, the drummer, sat amongst assorted beer barrels with a pair of drumsticks resting against his leg, waiting to play, as soon as the flighty ones had settled.

"Don't take a mind to it," Belle was saying.

"How can I not? Maybe you would be better off on your own."

"Whistle, stop it."

"I should go back to being a street balladeer."

"I said no to Hollingshead, didn't I?"

"But you said you would bear in mind his offer for the future."

Belle reared up to full height, petite in stature but somehow metropolitan policeman in spirit.

"I had to keep from offending him. He could just as easy ruin us as promote our cause. Oh, but that's not good enough for you. If you think I shows bad judgement and wants to leave, well there ain't nothing stopping you shifting your lazy arse up those stairs and out into the big, wide world."

"You three coping with life?"

I tossed this question from the stairs, hoping to disperse any artistic tensions.

"Hollingshead has offered work, at the Adelphi," moaned Whistle.

"That's heartening news."

"But only for Belle. They don't want me, and they certainly don't want Long Tom."

"Oi," objected Long Tom. "They either want you or they don't. When it comes down to it, there ain't no gradations of not being wanted."

"Take no notice," comes Belle in her decisive voice. "We have bigger fish to catch than Hollingshead."

"Bigger than Hollingshead?"

I had to ask this question, seeing as Hollingshead was the swankiest promoter this side of Drury Lane.

"Yes," said Belle glaring at me.

As always, I felt the impressiveness of Belle's determination. She's a very pretty girl, her looks a matter of hard delicacy, with lemon-white hair all gentle around upright shoulders. She's as sweet as ice cream, but also has a chilly sharpness that's an equal attribute of ice cream. Her attractiveness is like a stage costume. Most girls identify with their looks. Not Belle - she is aware that they are a weapon, which could just as easily harm the user as defeat an enemy.

"Now let's play that krooman thing again," demanded Belle of her partner.

"What's the point?" moaned Whistle.

I looked towards Long Tom sitting amongst the barrels. He had been coming for a while now, having learned his drumming on the pearly harvest-festival street marches. On the march, he only had one drum, which for a man of his deep waters was not enough. He had been drinking one day in the Prince of Denmark and heard faint sounds of rehearsal. Now he sat on a barstool amongst barrels arranged about him, banging upon them as Belle and Whistle played. Letting him do this had started out as an act of musical charity to a quiet boy who loved to hit things. Over time it had become a deal more than that. I joined up in a similar way. A few months previously, whilst helping Vince with necessary brewery correspondence, the strains of driving music had come up to me. On that day I descended down to the cellar and proffered words, starting as conversation, before turning into songs.

"Play the kroomen thing for Tim," demanded Belle. "See if he can get any words."

"But you have been offered the Adelphi," moaned Whistle.

"Forget the Adelphi. Just play the new tune."

Then I heard a thing that made me lift my head up from the weary slump it had fallen into. It started with Long Tom hitting some tinkling beats on an empty beer bottle, after which, with sweeping hands, his sticks began striking the barrels about him. One hand skittled away at a one-and-two thing in quick, regular groups of eight; the other jumped on some of these beats here and there, while his foot kicked a big thump - single then double, then back to single again. The sum of all these concussions was a sound predictable as Thames tides, but still very difficult to hold in your head because the sound kept darting away from where you could keep a grip on it. Regular yet mischievous, the beat went round and round in a way that made a body want to move. Belle contributed chords off the beat, followed by Whistle who started on a melody that I can only describe as bendy.

As the music gathered, I thought of the kroomen.

Kroomen are Navy coves from Africa, on the West African Station mostly. We would sometimes run into them on the docks, toting cargo and singing songs. I could almost see Jack Upside Down of HMS Neptune and hear his chocolate voice. Jack and his kroo - Half Dollar, John Boo, Poor Fella - they would turn any lumber into drums, just like Long Tom was doing now with barrels.

Words started to form in my mind, about a woman I'd met one time upstairs when I was working up excise correspondence for Vince. From a pocket, I pulled a piece of paper and scrap of Cumberland lead pencil, provided by Almanac for moments of inspiration. Thus equipped, I scribbled some lines about a music hall woman, who I once met in a beer-smelling taproom in Wapping.

I've just about enough of a singing voice to get the words out and show how they might work when a proper singer, such as Whistle or Belle took over singing duties. It was while thus occupied that someone appeared at the top of the stairs. This man was a very striking popinjay, somewhere halfway between an English gentleman and an Indian emperor. He tossed back dark locks of hair, a gesture which both announced his arrival and demonstrated that we were worthy of his attention.

"Good afternoon."

Music stuttered to a halt. We all gazed up in confusion at this apparition.

"Are you lost?" asked Belle, the first to pull herself together.

"No, I am exactly where I intend to be. My name is Eddie Mulsara, and I have been hearing interesting things about you."

"You have?" There was surprise in Belle's voice.

"Yes, from Hollingshead."

Whistle's body slumped over his guitar.

"Oh great. He's come back to throw Belle over his shoulder and take her off to a better life."

"Nobody's throwing me over their shoulder."

This was a statement I had no trouble believing.

Eddie Mulsara commenced to flounce down the stairs.

"I used to work with Hollingshead, but that temporary arrangement is at an end. In fact it was a means to an end, the nature of which I hope I now see before me."

By now, this figure from colonial fairy tale was standing amongst us.

"So you must be Belle and Whistle."

"Hollingshead said he only wanted Belle," reiterated Whistle.

"As I said, I don't work with him anymore. Our arrangement came to an end as soon as I heard about you."

"You, as in all of us?" quizzed Whistle.

"You must be Tom," said Eddie looking in our drummer's direction, a man who currently appeared glad of the barrels standing between him and this wholly unexpected visitor. "And who is this tatty little fellow?"

"That's Tim," declared Belle, in a tone that suggested she would defend me if necessary. "He writes our words."

"Well, Tim, Hollingshead didn't mention you, but suffice to say, I heard your song from the top of the stairs, which is why I came down them. Now I would like you to play it again, and I will do the singing."

At this point, there was a nonverbal conference amongst us of eyes meeting eyes. Belle was, once again, the first to regain her presence of mind.

"You want to sing?"

"Yes. Then, I want to offer you all a job. But let's sing first."

"Alright, you can have a go, as you've offered."

My feeling was that Belle said this mainly to wind up Whistle, who did not have time to object because Long Tom, only truly happy while drumming, had already started that introductory tinkling on the beer bottle. Now with the fuse lit, it was inevitable that Belle came in with those off-the-beat chords, Whistle taking up the swaggering, bendy section. This time Eddie sang the words, in what was immediately apparent as a prime voice. There was real bite to it, some rasp to go with clarity. After only hearing my words once, he sang through the entire verse I'd written.

> I met her in a beer-smelling taproom down in Wapping
> She suggested things that I had not yet tried
> She looked quite young but I think she was much older
> It's took three years to get her off my mind
> She's a music, music, music hall woman
> Gimme, gimme, gimme the music hall blues

"No offence to Tim," said Belle, at the end of the verse, "but that was proper singing."

"I never laid claim to being a singer," I objected.

"Tim, we know that," said Belle with smart, ice cream sweetness. "You are the man for words."

"I can help you, and not just with the singing," declared Eddie.

"So what are you offering?" asked Belle.

"Ah, now that's complicated. It's difficult to give details, beyond the fact that it is your use of kroo music that we are interested in."

"Who's we?" asked Whistle.

"I can't tell you, not yet anyway."

"We have to know what we're getting into," insisted Belle.

"There's many a sad fate that can befall a desperate

musician in this town," was Whistle's opinion.

"This offer involves music. It does not involve any activity where Mr Whistle is required, for example, to shed his clothes."

Long Tom tittered at this, and gave a little beat on one of the barrels to lend humour to the moment.

"We are not accepting any job offer without knowing what it is." This was Belle looking after our interests. "We are not that needful."

"And we do our own singing," added Whistle.

"I'm just saying that I know people who can help. This kroomen approach is just what we are looking for. I'm convinced. There are people who will want this. I'm not trying to sell you a dog here."

"Maybe we should just forget it and play music hall," moaned Whistle.

At this Belle went as mad as hops with Whistle. It was disappointing that I had to leave at this point, having promised Rawbone before I parted from him, that I would attend a meeting about Her Majesty's wretched lost ring. As well as the fun of seeing Whistle roasted, I was interested in this unexpected visitor and his surprise of an offer. Now maybe we needed to take a chance. Perhaps Eddie did have something that might help. He really had sung my words with justice. And if he wasn't forthcoming about the details of his proposition, so what? There are lots of secrets in the East End, lots of protection of sources of capital, and plain old drama for the sake of drama.

"Eddie, I have to go, but we're interested."

This was my intended casual remark. It was not received as such by Belle who had some attention left over from ripping Whistle, to be offended by my presumption of authority.

"Oh we are, are we?" she breathed.

Whistle had the presence of mind to adopt a stance of annoyance sent in your narrator's direction, pleased that Tim's high-handedness had turned Belle's treatment away from him.

"He's taking on," smarmed Whistle, uniting against an exterior enemy.

Belle had knuckles on hips.

"We are not getting into something we know nothing about. You go on to your appointment, Tim. Leave decisions to us."

It was time to depart. Making for the stair, I heard Eddie calling out some parting information.

"Dear boy, if you need to reach me, I can generally be found at Rules Restaurant, Maiden Lane, between eight and nine of an evening."

Not much registering these words, I dashed back up to the Prince of Denmark, dodged through the bar and risked my life once again in Grace's Alley.

CHAPTER 4

Rosemary Lane is just east of the Tower, near St Katherine's Docks. Sailors live in Rosemary Lane, which also means that sailors don't live there. That's because they are either drowned, or away voyaging on their wormy ships waiting to drown. A place where sailors live is really a place where women live, organising things better than men do. And the other thing to bear in mind on this topic is that Rosemary Lane is not respectable, which means the women don't have to worry about being modest, quiet and chaste. So put two things together - lack of men, who are away at sea, combined with freedom from the strictures of respectability - and that's when you get the women stepping forward, as they did in Sparta, so Almanac tells me. Ever hear of the Sleepe sisters and their fan-making business down Cheapside? Well there were a lot of ladies like that on Rosemary Lane, running the rag trades, the nut and orange sellers, the pure finders. Old Ma runs an appreciable portion of London's toshing.

Anyhow, I was at Old Ma's place, just off Rosemary Lane in Blue Anchor Yard. We were waiting for Boggo. The reason for this meeting had been passed to us by our contact at Buckingham Palace. It was Forbes who explained that the Rat and Mole Destroyer was trying to win royal favour. Her Majesty hates rats, moles, and everything to do with them, which includes the Official Destroyer. Boggo planned to turn around his reputation in the eyes of the Queen with tosher help. It seems that through a fog of substituted polite words relating to the royal khazis, Boggo had ascertained that Her Majesty last saw the lost ring in her Buckingham Palace bathroom. That meant it probably went down a plughole. The idea of a plughole is a source of despair for most, but not for Boggo. Through his knowledge of rats, sketchy as it seems to be, he at least knows that when something goes down a plughole it does not vanish from the face of the Earth. Sometimes it only goes a few hundred yards before lodging somewhere. To get such a lost item back, I understand why you might think that he would go to the flushers. They are official men, equipped with keys and uniforms. But it's not wise to take notice of fancy keys and uniforms. Flushers only know their way to the sluices. Their knowledge is in the flushing of things further away. Toshers know how to get things back. It must have given Boggo pain when he realised he would have to go and see Old Ma. But if he wanted the glory of recovering that ring, an interview with Old Ma was his reckoning.

Anyhow, it was towards evening. There were a lot of young-uns ready to help on lookout. One of those little ones careened into Blue Anchor Yard, shouting that Boggo was on his way. Evidently, our high and mighty rodent catcher was approaching through the clothing market, where fashions of yesteryear and people that folks used to be, now hung on a hook waiting for someone else to take them up and live their lives all over again. The market always gives a feeling that clothes you have on your person are for sale. You are just borrowing them for purposes of display.

"He's a coming," was the cry. "He's wearing a prime pair of boots."

And so he was, the dust of Rosemary Lane sitting hazy-like on the shine of those Balmorals as they swung along. This was Boggo come to see Old Ma.

Boggo strutted below the broken arch leading into Blue Anchor Yard. Watching him reminded me of a time rowing on the river with Rawbone. Passing the Tower, we saw Traitors'

Gate.

"Look, lad," Rawbone had said. "That's Traitors' Gate. See how they built it just above the water, so the castle can look down upon the poor souls who enter there."

Traitors' Gate makes people feel small. Blue Anchor Yard has its own Traitors' Gate, and Boggo was walking through it, poor fool. He was his very own Mary Queen of Scots.

Old Ma gazed upon Boggo from a spongy gallery. The various posts and pillars holding this structure aloft would have interested those Greeks who knew about strange geometry.

"Aren't we good enough for you these days, Boggo?" called Old Ma from over the rail, which I hoped she'd avoid leaning against.

The restraint of her words surprised me. She could have had Boggo poured into the Thames if she wanted.

"Don't be like that, Ma," answered Boggo, an ingratiating smile on his upturned face. Our foreshortening, lofty viewpoint made it appear that a pair of Balmorals protruded directly from a well-fed generosity of waist.

"If you are fortunate in this life, you should bring that fortune back to the place you were made."

"I'm here now, good lady. I'm here to ask for help, not for me but for Our Queen. She has lost something that I suspect is in the sewers. Assist me and I will endeavour to persuade the Metropolitan Board of Works that your toshers provide a valuable service in keeping the sewers clear of debris."

"This coming from you who is trying to close us down?"

"The Board of Works has the best of intentions, madam. Times are changing for us all, but I might be able to get you a place in London's future."

Boggo made it sound as though toshing was about to become a career, which a gentleman might choose in preference to the Law or the Church. He really wanted to turn us all into flushers. Why wasn't Ma emptying the slops on his head?

They talked back and fore. Boggo thought he had Ma daunted, and Ma let him believe that. She even sighed after the name of her dearly departed husband – lost these ten years to the rocks of Prussia Cove - whose opinion would be so helpful at this difficult moment. Old Ma worked a man so puffed up with himself that he had no idea. Once the talk was done, he marched away through our very own Traitors' Gate, into the gathering gloom of dusk no doubt feeling pleased with himself. Then, with Boggo Queen of Scots gone, the unusual look of doubt left Old Ma's face. Her features aligned themselves once again with her determined wrinkles, like compass needles swinging around to point the way we should go.

"Rawbone," she shrilled. "Get in here. I need to talk to you."

Of the conversation that followed, I could only hear its tone through the wall. If mudlarks found an old, discarded fiddle and bass viol lying on the Thames mud, and had a go at playing them, the resulting sound would mimic what I was hearing. It was the up and down of a bad duet.

This odd noise stopped. The door creaked open. Rawbone's face appeared, as full of grain and knots as the wood of the door itself.

"If you would be so kind as to step in, Tim."

"Who, me?"

"Get in 'ere, boy," screeched the upper registers of Old Ma's violin. I jumped to it.

Once inside, I saw Old Ma sat at her circular table of counsel. Gesturing for me to join her, she tugged on a pulley, which moved a duplex paraffin burner down over the table. Two flames flared within a semicircular, translucent, lavender shade, producing a bright pool of light, shutting out the world to our classified conversation. Who knows what items of domesticity lay in gloom beyond the light, what sideboards with bowls and jugs, what beds covered in lace bedspreads? Everything now focused on business. It was as though I sat in a great, dark space where the only reality was our topic of discussion.

"Interesting news about this ring, Tim."

"Yes, Ma. Are we going to try and find it?"

"We are, but first we need a measure of insurance. Now tell me, Tim, what do you think our chances are of finding her 'ighness's ring? Gawd bless her."

"Cast iron certainty, Ma."

"Stop it, boy. I don't need flattery. I have older, bigger, stronger men than you for that. Now, you are a good boy. You see things many don't. Tell me truthfully, what are the chances of finding Queenie's trinket?"

I took a glance towards Rawbone, whose gentle nod whispered reassurance. This gave me confidence to continue.

"Well, that's a tricky one and no mistake. We have to keep in mind that this is Buckingham Palace itself we are talking about. I hear they have the finest Thomas Crapper chinaware in the bathrooms, vitrified enamel and so on - powerful flush with an eight foot drop - plenty of water supplied by taps fitted directly to baths and basins, giving a lot of volume with a powerful down flow when the plugs are pulled. That means the chances of items travelling are increased. And anything getting into a centre flow will have been carried down the main a long ways, maybe into the interceptor already, maybe even dumping into the Thames herself, where of course only Janie's ghost would find it."

Rawbone looked heavenward at my mention of our patron saint of toshers, who I have to say is probably as made-up as old Father Nick himself.

"So, what are the chances?" asked Old Ma, leaning forward, her face looming in the bubble of hectic gas light, carbuncles casting carbuncle shadows.

"In reality, maybe as low as eight to one."

It made me feel important to be using terms of the turf. I thought they were fitting for the occasion. Old Ma had never consulted me on an important matter of policy before, though I had often read *The Enquirer* to her.

"I agree. Those odds are too long for something like this. I've heard through Forbes that the reward for finding this ring is substantial, and we cannot have eight to one against as our best chance. So we need to improve those odds to a dead certainty."

"We can only do our best, Ma. The flush, the flow..."

"Never mind about all that. What I am talking about doesn't worry itself with no flushing. I want us to make a ring. Blackwell will take the commission."

"Blackwell? Not the Blackwell as makes birdcages, razors, red-herring toasters, and trivets?"

"Those are just his bulk lines. He also makes art pieces and jewellery, which looks expensive but usually ain't, leastwise not as expensive as the original. That is his true love, his deepest artistry and highest calling. He will make us a counterfeit, so that not even the Queen herself will know the difference. We will securely place this ring somewhere below the palace, and by the chances of all the fates, we will of course find it in our search. This is the ring that Rawbone gives to Boggo. It will be made slightly too big for the Queen's finger - just a little mind so she doesn't notice - but enough for it to slip off again at some point in the future so we can go through this whole thing again. That will keep Boggo in our pocket, seeing as he needs us to find the lost items of his careless mistress."

I looked at Old Ma in awe.

"Aye, lad, good isn't it?" said Rawbone. "But that's not the best of it."

Rawbone glanced towards Old Ma in a way that asked if he could deliver the punchline. She looked back in a way that said the punchline was all his, due to his long and faithful service.

"Once the transaction with Blackwell's ring is complete, we will start looking for the real ring in earnest. If it's truly lost, then there's no skin off anyone's nose. We will still be well ahead. If we do find it, our contacts abroad will pay a very pretty price."

So this is how the world works, I thought to myself. I might as well have been sitting with the viceroy of India himself, up in his residence on a mountaintop at Simla making things happen across the subcontinent.

"That is a great plan, Ma. Is it me you want for going after the ring? If so, there's others with more experience in the tunnels of that area."

"Nay, Lad," said Rawbone, doing the answering when it came to his own area of expertise. "Toshing has only been a support of your studies. It's your knowledge about reading and documents an' libraries that we need. We would use Almanac himself for a job of this importance, but he is not a well man. Asking for his recommendation, he said it had to be you. You will be the one writing to the original maker of the Queen's ring under the guise of The British Museum, wishing to preserve its details for posterity. You must find out what the ring looked like and give a precise description to Blackwell. That's your job, and you must work quickly. We have told Blackwell he can expect specifications this coming Friday."

Yet again, I was being asked to write something I did not really want to write. At least this commission was better than labouring on royal scandal sheets, or pamphlets about the evils of toshing. I told myself that a lot of money could come out of this caper, which could all go into my song writing. It's amazing how much cold reality goes into making dreams come true.

CHAPTER 5

I rushed over to Almanac's place, donned my good suit which I kept at his chambers and went to my task at the British Library in Bloomsbury. It was Almanac who had got me a ticket, allowing me to enter this great, domed space, lifting the very sky on its shoulders. By some magic the library's interior had more space than London outside it, which was no doubt necessary if you are obliged to house all these books. Volume after volume went round in concentric orbits one above the other, ever upwards in great rings of learning. Rings seemed to be the theme for today. That was interesting. And so my undisciplined mind began thinking of possible words for a song, about circles and spirals and wheels within wheels.

Leave that, I demanded of myself. It's research you're here to pursue.

There were so many books that they made me feel small in both body and spirit. No one could read more than a small fraction. The fraction I looked at involved jewellers to the Queen. Indexes were very useful, speeding me along, my finger running down the Vs until I reached Victoria. In this way, I found the makers of a ring for a royal personage named Her Royal Highness Victoria, given to her by Albert, who was also credited with the design. Prince Albert apparently did a lot of jewellery designing, which was a surprise to me. The ring maker was a man named Joseph Kitching. Forbes had provided a sheet of creamy, Buckingham Palace paper. Centred close to the upper edge was a red shield, topped with a crown. From each side a lion and unicorn scrapped over shield and crown spoils. After practice on the back of an old advertising bill for Colman's Mustard, I proceeded to compose my letter on the lovely, royal canvas, asking if Mr Kitching would be so kind as to produce drawings for a ring recently lost by Her Royal Highness Victoria, so that the design could be accurately recorded at the museum.

I wrote in the way Almanac had taught me for this sort of purpose. He called it using the passive, which involved pretending my words were appearing out of a big machine rather than a living person sitting at a desk with a pen. I said a ring had been lost, as though it had kind of lost itself, rather than any person doing the losing. A record has to be made, suggesting sheets of paper covering themselves with words. Gratitude for this service was to be passed along, as though the good wishes had a life of their own. Feeling more like a shadow than a writer, I put my letter in an envelope, furnishing it with Kitching's address. Then it was a matter of hurrying out into Great Russell Street, where a courier atop a horse waited to take the letter to Kitching's London premises.

Mr Kitching was nothing if not efficient. After taking receipt at Buckingham Palace, Forbes dropped off a package at Almanac's parlour the following day. All seemed in order. We had drawings, dimensions, side notes, numbers of carats, addresses of diamond mines in Australia. I now knew the difference between a round brilliant cut and a princess cut. Albert had gone for the princess cut, which was fitting for someone of his royal persuasion.

Receiving word from Almanac, I went straight to Blackwell's workshop. This meant heading east of Rosemary Lane into Millwall, that garishly pigmented part of London where you find the paint factories. Chimney smoke poured here in chalky vermillion, Spanish blue, bitter lemon yellow, thunderstorm green, and shepherd's warning red. The blue looked as pure as summer skies, until you wandered into that azure effusion, to find your skin burning on your outsides and your lungs afire on your insides. The pigeons, tinted by flight through coloured smoke, are the sort of birds that might flutter by the glassy eyes of Balzac who, Almanac tells me, used to try to help his writing by sticking his head in a barrel of rotting apples and taking deep breaths. I have already resolved not to use that method in my own writing, so there's no need to warn me against it.

The street I walked down had an orange hue, as though sunsets had settled into dust beneath my feet. Almanac's directions led to a long brick building, where each section of the facade stood alternately behind and then proud of its neighbour. The windows were reminiscent of a prison hulk, deep set, rectangular, with an arched upper edge. It is not natural to walk into a place that looks like a building to be escaped from, but that is what I forced myself to do.

Inside were dark, tropical-feeling rooms, by turns junk shop, museum and smithy. Before me was a lump of something that was half rock, half woman with an ornate hair styling. She stood on a bench in a row of similar women, each striking a different pose. There were so many odd objects crowding in on my attention - Italianate pictures, vases, candlesticks, three violins rendered in varnish so perfect that the wood appeared to have turned to crystal. On the wall, in shadow, I saw suspended a couple of strange looking guitars, thinner in the body than usual. I would have looked closer, but this was not a time to poke around.

Straying deeper into the workshop's gloomy fastness, a bust of American president George Washington stared from a bench, half his alabaster face lit vermilion by hungry forge fire. Turning towards this source of heat and light, I beheld flames over which seethed a steel beaker of molten liquid, a white-yellow colour. I took a few steps back, driven into retreat by skin-prickling radiance, and the leathered expression of the hell-puddle's scorched guardian. His shading of dark hair, combed in a wet sort of way, glittered with oily efflorescence. The fire's infernal glow festered on black-glass goggles clamped across a face glowing like the Man in the Moon, if the moon had caught fire. My back bumped up against a marble lady in gauzy, marble clothing. This was as far as retreat could go, which meant there was no choice but to face the twitchy, hell-puddle man.

A huge but cringing youth lumbered into the area of incandescence, towering over his shrunken, flaming captain.

"I've prepared the stone, for the bust of Nefatiti's daughter."

"About time, Smalt. Now get some filler ready for the Van Dyke. Use more gypsum this time. More gypsum."

"Of course, Mr Blackwell."

"Mr Blackwell?" I ventured.

"Are you the boy, Tim? I was expecting Almanac."

Smalt shuffled away, concentrating on his instructions:

"More gypsum, more gypsum."

"Mr Almanac is indisposed, sir. I have come in his stead."

"What is it that he wants? All I hear is rumours. It's the facts I need."

"If you please, sir."

I indicated a bench off to one side, outside the fire's death zone. Blackwell put down his implements in the manner of a bookish person interrupted in their reading of a good novel. Divested of goggles and tongs, he moved to the bench, moving aside a plaster head of a Roman senator wearing a garland, to make room for documents I laid, as Forbes might lay out silver cutlery and Russian Blue china at the palace. I took my time, was methodical, and tried to invest the whole thing with a flourish of theatre. Blackwell wasn't looking at my display. He kept his eyes on me. This was unnerving. By the time I got to the documents about diamond mines, I just dumped them on the table like they were some old bills. Only then did Blackwell look down at my offerings, his calloused hands gentle and precise as they turned pages and studied drawings.

"A royal ring?"

"Yes, sir."

"I see. This will be interesting, and expensive."

"We only need a fake, sir."

"Only a fake?" he spat.

"I just meant we didn't need a real one."

"Not a real one? Smalt!"

The enormous, cringing boy cringed and lumbered back into his master's presence.

"Yes, Mr Blackwell?"

"Smalt, if you would be so kind as to take this visitor and throw him in the Thames."

"Of course, sir."

The grip on my upper arm felt like the sort of clench that would be more comfortable on the haft of a hammer sending sparks from hot metal.

"You don't understand. I meant no offence."

"The Thames, Smalt. Near the effluent outflow."

"Yes, sir."

I am not a street scrapper and there was nothing I could do to resist a smith's apprentice. He dragged me into a courtyard where the dust of painted sunset hung diaphanous and tiffany.

"Old Ma will hear of this," I squeaked.

"Old Ma?" repeated Smalt. "She won't 'elp you. But maybe I can."

"You can?"

Once he had stood me against the courtyard wall, Smalt shook me free of his grasp, like I was sticky flypaper.

"You little fool, calling the master's work a fake. What you thinking?"

"I was thinking, oh I don't know, that I had come here to order a fake ring."

"There you go again." Smalt snapped a look over his shoulder. "Listen to me. You'll only have one more chance, and I'm only helping you because you got a mate of mine a place as cabin boy by writing up his particulars in a letter for him. You are Tim the writer, ain't you?"

"Well, I'm called Tim and can write."

"I've always wondered; from whence do you writers get your ideas?"

"Oh, you know, here and there."

"Well, anyways. Gordy was that pleased with his particulars. So now, you give your ears to me, understand. I know the master, and I know such as he wants this commission. But he won't be made a fool of, not for nothing, not for Old Ma, or Almanac, or nobody. So if you want to stay on dry land, you listen good. Do not call the master's work a fake, or not real, or pretend, or anything of that nature. His work is exactly as prime as the real thing, the only difference being it has not been blessed by touch of a finger which 'appens to belong to a royal, or a captain of industry and the like. Don't you know that sometimes the only difference between a trinket and a piece of value is him or her who owned it. Do you see?"

"I think I do, Smalt."

"The Queen herself, serves as an example. She has shiny pebbles from a beach near Osbourne House on the Isle of Wight. Pebbles! From a beach, polished up a bit. Them pebbles are worth something. We even prepared a few of our own."

"I didn't know."

"Now this here ring you're talking about is no pebble. It's proper valuable, and with something like that you got an A and a B of a choice. You can either make like to the original, as close as possible, using original materials. That's A. Or B, you can make it look good, but using inferior materials for those lacking monetary means. If B is your aim, there is still no grounds for looking down your nose at the master's work, because it's with B that he has to employ his most profound real high arts. It is now that he has to lift lesser materials up to a state of grace, so that glass glitters like diamonds. It's more difficult to make glass glitter like diamonds then to make diamonds glitter like diamonds. That's because diamonds is already diamonds, while glass has to be coaxed and encouraged and forced to be diamonds. Do you see?"

"I do. I'm very sorry."

"Now, I know the master only threw you out because you made him do it. If I take you back now and you grovel and abase yourself and make up to him as if he was as worthy as Peter Fabergé himself, which he is, then you might still have a chance."

"Thank you, Smalt."

Once again my upper arm became the haft of a blacksmith's tool as Smalt bundled me back into the workshop's shades. We entered just as Blackwell, with the help of long tongs, poured what looked like a portion of Krakatoa lava into an intricate mould. While his concentration did not leave his work, he had a piece of attention, like a turning of scrap metal, left over to observe Smalt's approach.

"Is he not in the Thames yet, boy?"

"He has something to say to you, sir. Begging your pardon, but he has assisted a few mates with the writing up of our letters of introduction and is known to me as a decent fellow. After we had a talk, I think he sees where he was in the wrong."

"I do, sir. I really do."

"This is presumptuous of you, Smalt."

"I know, sir. Begging your pardon, sir."

"I apologise for failing to give your work the respect it most certainly deserves."

"Tell me, why do they send a boy to me? Why does Almanac not come, or Old Ma herself?"

"Almanac is not well, and Old Ma's legs trouble her, sir. They were too respectful of your time to ask you to come to Blue Anchor Yard. For an administrative chore, it is best someone like me comes along. I am but a messenger, who is as nothing compared to those who send messages or receive them."

Blackwell looked borderline amused by this.

"Have you the money for payment? This job won't be cheap. From what I hear toshing is not the business it used to be."

"It is true we are struggling with Boggo and his friends at the Board of Works, who seem to think it is in our best interest to run us out. However, we think finding this ring for Boggo will give us a hold over him."

Blackwell nodded in a calculated way, as though he were First Lord of the Treasury weighing up pros and cons related to invading some unsuspecting country.

"So you can pay, in advance?"

"We can pay. The reward is substantial. I believe a loan has been taken out against it. Pearlie funds are also involved. I just have to let Old Ma know that you are happy to take the commission and remittance will follow this evening."

"Yes, I have already seen the figure for the reward. You'll get a ring, which it will take someone trained to spot. And here's the thing. This piece is from Kitching. I have an agreement going with someone in his workshop. If Kitching is asked to verify, then my man will do that verifying in a way suited to us."

Blackwell turned his attention back to a broach solidifying into something that might sit on ladies' blouses for a thousand years.

"You will have the piece by Tuesday night."

I knew this was the end of our interview and there would be no pleasantries.

Smalt acted as escort back to the orange-dusted street.

"Nicely played, Tim. But remember one thing, you must pay on the nose. Any problems with that and you won't have me to save you from the river."

CHAPTER 6

After all my research at the British Museum and the nerve-wracking haggling at Blackwell's, it felt good to be under London's streets again. Rawbone had rowed us to our point of embarkation. You'll forgive me if I'm not too specific, but I'll just say Vauxhall Bridge, and allow you to sketch in your mind the general area of London where our operations lay. It is near Vauxhall Bridge that we have our own private entrance to the King's Scholars' Pond Sewer. The King's Scholars' is as grand as its name. The British Museum Reading Room made an upwards direction seem like a big thing. The sewers do the same for along-ways. Truly, the distance of a tunnel sweeping into a dark distance is something I never get used to. Everything carries the eye, because all is designed in a curving way to carry water.

The King's Scholars' begins at the Thames as a stretched out arch. Some tunnels are shaped like an egg, some are a circle; this one is more of a lozenge, a lozenge shaped chamber of immense longways dimensions. So beautiful is it that the dangers are difficult to remember. I imagine tropical jungles must be like this, full of lovely trees and flowers and tigers, dangerous but breathtaking all the same.

In toshing terms our journey was relatively easy. The chamber allowed us to walk upright, following what used to be a river, called the Tyburn, now a grey stream confined to a concrete channel running along the sewer floor. In bubbles of light from our lanterns, we followed old Tyburn until it turned away into its own tunnel. Some distance beyond the Tyburn junction, progress became dryer underfoot as a cross tunnel intercepted the flow, taking it away towards one of those new estuary pumping stations.

We were now close to Victoria, hearing the low rumble of trains somewhere above our heads. This was one of the thrills of toshing for me. All those people thronging familiar thoroughfares, who have no idea of what lies below their feet. We can walk for miles just out of sight of their doings and lives. You really could make up a song about it. Maybe somebody will one day.

Beyond Victoria, the tunnel becomes a circle of orange and yellow brick, smooth orange below your feet to take the flow, yellow overhead. Following this orange and yellow brick road, we approached tunnels serving the palace. Here we ran into a familiar problem, the details of which I am not comfortable to go into. The Royal Family might not mean much to me, but I don't wish to cause difficulties for any potential publisher of this story, by giving away aspects of national security. Suffice to say this section always scares me, when rats, gasses and floods don't really. I always feel I can get out. But in this section we only proceed courtesy of our friends upstairs who have provided keys. There is always a worry that the flushers will come up behind us and change what we have adapted.

We passed the point of no return and carried on, knowing now that we were directly below Buckingham Palace. It tends to be dry here, with flow mainly coming from the royal source. Of course, what comes down looks just like what you'd get anywhere. Almanac once told me about a patterer, a former churchman, who was fond of impressing upon his congregation that everyone was the same in the eyes of God. One day he realised rich quality in his pews did not believe this. He came to us soon after. The sewers remind me of a cathedral on its side; and believe me, down here you see that everyone really is the same.

Now we had to place the ring, but where and how? It was

necessary to find a hiding place that we knew we could find again, even if flood intervened. Fake as it was, we had paid a great deal of money for this ring and could not risk losing it.

Rawbone squatted down, so as to be close to smooth, orange brick work.

"Here we go then, Tim."

Rawbone took the ring from his pocket and made it fast in a small cavity, using a wedge-shaped piece of cement. To a superficial gaze, the ring now looked to be lodged by the force of change and tide. It would remain secure, until a good pull freed it when the time came. By stages Rawbone straightened up, looking around, fixing the place in his mind.

"It's done. We are in it now, Tim. There's no going back. We have spent too much money for one thing."

His lamp, which I had held low to help his work, illuminated Rawbone's features from the wrong way round. It was not a pleasing effect. I am not superstitious as many are down here, but seeing Rawbone like that did not give me a good feeling. But why should I feel thus, when the plan seemed to be working well. A gang would be back the following night and would know just where to look. Then the ring would make its way into our hands back at Old Ma's and thence to Boggo. We'd get our reward and gain a hold over him. With my share, I could maybe take a few months to work on songs, to the exclusion of worldly concerns.

Such were my hopes the following evening, as we waited under Old Ma's duplex paraffin burner, pulled down over the table. It was a volatile gathering of people in that pool of light, brought together by circumstance, like sullen bags of cordite which happened to be stored in a magazine waiting to explode in a gun far above our heads. There was Old Ma, Almanac, your narrator, Boggo and Rawbone. We waited now for one of Rawbone's most trusted lieutenants - Angus the Drop, so called I believe because early in his career, he dropped his day's sewer findings into the Thames by accident. He had never been allowed to forget it. So often we are defined by the few things we do wrong rather than the many things we do right.

Rawbone, Old Ma and Almanac were talking in low voices. None of them appeared keen to converse with Boggo, who had just been bragging about his forethought in sending one of his men in with Angus to make sure there was no 'funny business'. Old Ma admitted that it was no good trying to get one over on the Royal Rat and Mole Destroyer.

After puffing himself up in this way, Boggo turned to me.

"So what are you doing here, Tim? Isn't this a job for your elders and betters?"

"Mr Almanac said you wanted someone to write up your triumph in finding the ring. Well that's me."

"Good lad. But for security reasons, if Angus says anything about the nature of safeguards down there, then you are to mention none of that."

"No, Mr Weedy."

"While we wait, young Tim, let me ask, have you considered my proposal?"

I looked with trepidation towards Old Ma and Rawbone, knowing that they must have heard. And Rawbone knew to what Boggo was referring - the offer to write a book about the miserable, subhuman life of toshers, with further appendices on the wretched existence of finders and costers. Boggo hadn't tried to talk in a private manner. He wanted everyone present to be aware, no doubt to antagonise them when they couldn't do much about it.

"The boy will not be working for you," croaked Rawbone in an ominous fashion. "We don't need nobody making him write any lies about us."

"But is it lies, Rawbone? You know as well as I do how hard the street lives are. As pearl king, you give money to vulnerables and see their plight first hand. You should know the hardness of this kind of life."

"So your answer is to take away our livelihoods and make us all vulnerables? What kind of solution is that? It's all very well for you and your fancy Spring Gardens friends to bring light to the benighted, but where are we all going to work if you take away our trades?"

"Rawbone, those trades themselves are the problem."

"Is that right? Good luck finding new jobs in fancy offices for all our people. Most of them wouldn't want that work even if you offered it them. You are living in a dream world where you is your very own hero. I declare, if we wasn't sitting here..."

"Enough," barked Old Ma. The combatants subsided into silence. Boggo turned his attention back to me, picking on the weakest of the herd I suppose.

"So if you don't come and write for me, who will you write for?"

"We got that organised," growled Almanac.

"Scandal sheets, is it?" scoffed Boggo. "I think the boy is worth more than that."

Almanac's face appeared mottled in a portentous sense. I use the word portentous because it's Almanac we're describing here, a man who has instilled in your narrator the value of a wide vocabulary. I use such a word to honour a man whose qualities were obscured in the eyes of some by his periodic rages, one of which I feared might now erupt if Boggo kept pushing it. Flora wasn't around with her rolling pin. Still, Old Ma was sitting next to him and she made Flora look like a flower girl. No wonder perhaps that Almanac remained in control, taking deep breaths in through those thickets that grew from each nostril.

"The boy wants to be a song writer," he said, trying I think to lighten the mood.

"Is that a job, then?" commented Old Ma with a cackle.

This stung me.

"I work with a double act called Belle and Whistle, Ma. We're quite good. I think one day we might even be famous. I will provide you with a ticket to one of our shows."

"You work with who?"

The vehemence of Boggo's question took me aback.

"Belle and Whistle, a music hall act. Have you heard of them?"

"You are not to work with them any longer."

"Don't tell the lad what to do," said Rawbone.

"Yes, leave the boy to make up his mind," wheezed Almanac, which I thought was a bit rich, considering his past resistance to the song writing idea.

"You are selling him short. You might be stuck in the past, but we at the Board of Works are looking ahead. This boy has the abilities we will be looking for in London's future."

After worrying about Almanac losing control, it was Rawbone who leapt to his feet, his chair flying backwards, out of the pool of gaslight into the outer darkness.

"Enough," roared Old Ma. "Rawbone, get your chair and sit down. Weedy, stop your talking and agitation. We all need this ring, and we are going to sit here until it arrives. Then we can go our separate ways. And no, Tim is not going to write nothing about our lives being bad. They're our lives and we will live them as we see fit. And if you want that ring, Boggo, you won't be arguing."

The room lapsed into the sort of silence you sometimes get on Christmas Day, when people are trying to maintain peace and goodwill, in the face of all those other days of the year when peace and goodwill are low priority.

It wasn't long before Old Saint Nick arrived in the shape of Angus the Drop. He brought with him the rush, business and ammonia of the outside world, along with Boggo's wrecked-looking minion, all of which was a relief from the oppression we had been sitting through.

"Old Ma," said Angus with due respect.

"Angus, do you have something for me?"

"Well, we've had a time of it. This fella Boggo sent down with us - he insisted on standing to attention beside the royal outflow. He was rewarded by a generous slop of fresh sliding down the wall."

Boggo's man wilted beside Angus. He was the same character who had acted look out at The Grapes. It appeared as though the King's Scholars' had been a shock to him.

"Was there any funny business?" asked Boggo of his man.

"None that I noticed," replied a shaky voice.

"Angus," pressed Old Ma, "do you have the ring?"

"Yes we have it. Lodged in a loose joint it was. Just perfect. Couldn't have asked for nothing better. Janie was truly watching over me. 'Ere it is."

At this point, Angus hesitated, as though it would not be quite proper to toss his find around like an old copper coin. Since there was no velvet cushion available for the purposes of display, he had to confine himself to a careful placing upon the table, using finger tips of two hands.

It looked like there had been some initial cleaning, probably with the piece of rag tucked into Angus's belt.

I have never described the ring to you properly, an omission which must now be put right. In bright lamp light, the central stone looked almost black, when it was also a kind of blue. This is a colour I have only ever seen once before. It was when I went with Rawbone on a rowing job down to Hampton Court. In those elegant Thames reaches, royal gardens came right down to the river, across which preened a quantity of fantastical bird, which Rawbone identified as peacocks. Spots on their fan tail were the same colour as I'm trying to describe to you now, blue on the outside fading to inky black in the middle. Just where the blue becomes black, that is the colour of this stone, reproduced by Blackwell's skill. Why does a bird have a tail like that? Why do some ladies have rings like the one we now beheld? To show off I suppose.

Blackwell had done the job of a magician in creating this ring. The light of Old Ma's lamp refracted into its tiny, oceanic depths. I think it would fool anyone. Lady peacocks would probably take that central stone off with them to their nests in the belief that they had found a baby peacock.

"This is not the ring," said Boggo.

There was an awful ensuing silence.

"What you mean?" snapped Rawbone. "Of course it's the ring. Don't you try and cheat us, unless washing up as jetsam at Tilbury appeals."

"It would be unwise to threaten me, Rawbone. I am an agent of the Crown. If I fail to return safely to the palace, there will be redcoats down here to remind you of your place."

It was of course difficult to tell if this threat was real. Would redcoats really bother themselves to avenge Boggo's demise? On the other hand, the mystique of Crown, Government and State hung around this man like a mayoral chain.

"Now, what is this nonsense?" asked Old Ma, bringing diplomacy to proceedings. "Angus found that ring near the royal outflow. How can it not be the right one?"

"This is not the ring. Look, I have a picture of the correct one here."

Boggo placed upon the table what looked like a small suitcase done up in red leather, the lid embossed with a gold coat of arms, consisting of a crown atop an entwined rat and mole. This must be the official despatch box of the Rat and Mole Destroyer, created I suspected, at the direction of Boggo himself. Releasing two golden clasps, he lifted the lid and pulled out a sheet of paper. At this point I felt sorry for Boggo. He was referring to sheets of paper, when I had the British Library behind me.

"Here is an illustration from the royal archive."

Using one hand, Boggo swivelled the illustration, towards Old Ma, Rawbone and Almanac on the other side of the table. All eyes focused on a ring, which was certainly not the ring that sat on the table in front of us.

"I don't understand," I blurted.

"What is there to understand? It is not the Queen's ring. That's an end to it. I have wasted my time. As for the ring we have here, no other jewellery has been reported lost at the palace, which is kept under strict audit. This ring constitutes lost property recovered in the public sewer. It looks nice enough, maybe washed down from Mayfair. Under my powers as Rat and Mole Destroyer, I am obliged to take this for safekeeping until its rightful owner can be found. If it remains unclaimed from myself after a six month period, the item will be sold, with its monetary value going to the British Treasury."

"No!" yelled Old Ma. "Rawbone stop him!"

"Stand away from the Royal Rat and Mole Destroyer," roared Boggo. "Any attack on me would be an assault on the Crown, which could not happen without the severest of consequences."

Boggo, taking his time, returned his evidence to his ridiculous red case, our precious ring, made by Blackwell, going in after it, and the lid shutting on all.

"Good evening ladies and gentlemen. I'd like to say it's been a pleasure but it hasn't."

With that Boggo strutted out, the lackey scurrying after him.

"He's lying," cried Almanac, turning back to the table after watching Boggo disappear through the door. "Don't worry, I still have some contacts at the Inns of Court, old students from my time at Oxford. Tim, all you need to do is show me the entry for Queenie's ring in your book of reference and our case is water tight."

Nodding mutely, I reached into a canvas bag at my feet, pulling out the volume, which I had borrowed on my British Library readers' ticket. Laying it upon the table, I found the vital page.

"Here, look. This is the entry. See, a ring made by Prince Albert for Her Royal Highness, Victoria."

I jabbed at a line of text beside a perfect reproduction of our peacock-like chunk of jewellery. I read the entry again, feeling that it was saving me. A line of writing can save you. That's what I felt deep down, and that's what made me want to be a writer.

"Oh for the love of..."

Rawbone massaged his temples as though he would achieve the impossible and smooth out the lines there.

Something had gone wrong. I stood up, apparently to allow the others easier access to my reference book. In reality it already seemed like a good idea to start backing out.

There was a general groan around the room, combined with oaths from Old Ma, that to include in this book would only have given work to the Lord Chamberlain's censor's office.

"It says, Her Royal Highness, Victoria. That is the title referring to Princess Victoria, the Queen's eldest daughter. If it was the Queen, it would be, Her Majesty." Almanac's eyes were so intent on the bright page that he had not noticed my shuffling towards the door.

"Are you telling me," roared Old Ma, "that we made a ring for a princess because your genius pupil doesn't know the difference between highness and majesty?"

I knew there were good reasons to hate royalty. One of those reasons was their confusing use of names. Queen and princess, mother and daughter, both called Victoria. Everyone else seemed to know that Your Highness refers to a princess. Well forgive me for not knowing the difference between majesty and highness. I just wasn't up with royal titles. It was time to get out. Running down the spongy stairway outside Old Ma's chambers I wondered if I would ever see Blue Anchor Yard again.

CHAPTER 7

My mistake touched so many people, all those who had donated to pearlie funds, or invested in the Friendly Society. Now where would I go? Who was I outside Rosemary Lane? A great turning point had arrived in my life. In many ways all that I've told you so far has been preamble to my main story, which starts here.

I realised that your narrator had enjoyed the good life for too long and had lost sight of what was really important. Who cares about song writing dreams when poverty is at the door? If only I had accepted Almanac's advice about puff for patent medicines, fake love letters of Italian noblemen, or political tracts for the betterment of society. Lost and alone in London, any of those choices would have been heaven sent.

With every door closed against me, I recalled a possibility that might now be my only chance. Eddie Mulsara had offered work of an unknown nature. My mind clouded by fear and panic struggled to recall the place he mentioned, if I needed to find him. Be there between eight and nine o'clock. But what was the name he tossed around so casually? I had been unintentionally treacherous to my people. Now my own mind was treacherous to me. This is what happens upon breaking the most basic rules. That was it. Rules Restaurant, Maiden Lane.

Some sad street wandering was required to get through to that stated time of eight o'clock, announced to me by the bells of St Martin's. I debated whether it was best to arrive dead on eight, but then snarked at myself for thinking that I was in any position to consider the whys and wherefores of arriving fashionably late. This was survival, not social engagement. So there I stood, at eight o'clock, looking at scarlet canopies and plate glass windows, wondering how to get in.

A doorman spotted me, his outfit having a military bearing, fitting for a defender of doors.

"What are you up to, sir?"

I glanced around, wondering which sir he was addressing.

"Sorry. Are you talking to me?"

"This is how we address people at Rules, even the other staff."

"That's very polite."

There was something unexpected about this man's manner. While there was a crispness of uniform and the suggestion of violence if mobilised, this was tempered by hesitation in judgement, suggesting an appreciation that "sirs" came in all shapes and sizes.

"So, what are you about, sir? Do you have business here, or will I have to move you on?"

"I am here to see Mr Mulsara."

The doorman's stance was already upright. If possible, it became more inclined to the vertical, as though his feet might even leave the ground.

"If you could wait a moment, sir."

The doorman shimmered into his domain. Most of the wide window was an evening street in reflection, where two or three of me stood superimposed, all of them cold, small and alone. These ghostly Tims became mixed up with the spirit of a doorman re-emerging from restaurant shadow.

"If you would like to come with me."

And there I was, beyond the door, in a place that was all scarlet, yellow and glittering crystal. I wasn't exactly dressed for dinner, but no one seemed to mind. Smart and slip-shod were represented here, and both seemed worthy of business-like service. The doorman led to a booth where sat Eddie Mulsara.

There was rapid finishing of mouthful, emergency dabbing of lips with linen napkin. An open-palmed gesture offered me a place at the opposite bench. When it became possible, this offer was reinforced with words.

"Tim, good to see you. Please, sit."

"I had nowhere else to go."

"What has happened?"

"All I have to say is that I got majesty and highness muddled."

"That does sound serious. A significant lapse of etiquette. Well, don't worry. In bringing you here, your problem has become an opportunity."

Eddie took a nip of red wine, before placing his glass back down into a circular impression in the tablecloth. This perfect circle suggested a full-stop at the end of a sentence, paragraph, or even an entire chapter of my life.

"Often the biggest turning points arrive unexpectedly, don't you think, Tim? If you have run into difficulty, then I can give you a job. That job is to persuade your musician friends to accept my offer."

"I could try, but they want to know what they are getting into."

"Look, we'll talk about it in a while. First, I'm sure you want some refreshment."

"Maybe a couple of sausages and a cuppa tea would be welcome."

"No hot drinks and no beer. Those are the rules at Rules."

"I'll have whatever you say."

Another bottle of red wine ended up on the table. Unlike Almanac's bottle of porter, this wine very much had a label, with French words and calligraphy. I poured out a measure into a glass, even though as you might realise by now, drinking was not a thing with me. After the sausages disappeared, which didn't take long, my glass of ruby wine became a kind of totem serving to confirm that I now had some measure of belonging in this unknown place.

Eddie started asking me questions, probing the Victoria disaster. Then we moved on to my writing career. This conversation served to settle my nerves, because it suggested that at a moment of peril there was someone in the world who didn't want to see me in the Thames. I now felt confident enough to ask again about this job offer.

"Mr Mulsara," I said.

"It's Eddie."

"Eddie, I want to know what it is you propose..."

"Tim!"

"Belle!"

Further questions were impossible, because there she was, beside our booth, my friend Belle, her lovely pale hair curved around its margins, waving gentle against the collar of a black cloak. In that speechless moment, Belle's cloak spoke to me more eloquently than words. It was a garment which made me think of stewardesses coming tired off liners, once observed on the occasion of a trip to Liverpool docks with Rawbone. Those ladies wore cloaks that were proper, not in the way of narrow social milieu, rather in the way of a wide, professional world. Belle's cloak was similar, looking well in this restaurant. Behind Belle stood Whistle and Long Tom, as though a meeting had been arranged with prior times noted and verified.

"What are you doing here?" asked Belle.

"I've been thrown out of Blue Anchor Yard. What are you doing here?"

"It seems someone," snapped Whistle, "has told all the bookers in London to avoid us. And not only that. Our current digs are of the theatrical variety and we've been given notice there as well."

"Please," Eddie was saying, "all of you, take a seat and I will arrange something to eat and drink. Come, Mr Whistle, this is a restaurant not an ambush. Sit you down."

And so the booth was now me, Belle and Long Tom on one side sitting close together, Eddie and Whistle on the other, with a big gap between them.

Once we were all settled and Eddie had called for items of sustenance, I wondered at the position in which I found myself, wedged beside Belle on the inside of a booth in Rules Restaurant, as though there was no choice but to find myself in this totally unexpected place and situation. And of course I was obliged not to make any show of how pleasant it was to be lodged in a tight space with Belle. Any reference to that and it wouldn't be so nice anymore.

"So, Tim, I ask again; what are you doing here?" queried Belle, looking sideways and a little down at me.

"We need to cheer him up," said Eddie to fill my hesitation. "He's made some kind of etiquette foul."

"What you been up to, Tim?" asked Whistle, wary and surly. "Have you upset anyone important? Is it you who has got us banned and thrown out of our lodgings?"

This was worse than I thought. My terrible actions must have brought dishonour on my musical friends.

"I made a mistake. I'm sorry. But it is true, I have upset a lot of people, Old Ma included. Money was involved."

"Just tell us what happened," soothed Belle.

As it was her asking I had no defences, starting right in on the tale of Victoria's fake ring and the highness instead of majesty blunder. I finished by revealing how much money I had lost with my carelessness. This was greeted with sounds of physical pain, to stand in for the sting of moral shock.

"It's the costers who have blocked us then," was Whistle's assessment.

"I'm sure it ain't Tim's fault," declared Belle, in a way that suggested it was my fault, but she would defend me anyway.

"Come on now," said our host. "This is perfect. If you can't work anywhere else, then you are at least free to take up my offer."

It seemed almost disrespectful for Eddie to take my pain and use it for his positive outlook.

I saw Whistle's dark glare, formerly directed at me, now transform into nodding suspicion directed at Eddie.

"Isn't that odd? You offer us a job, then all of a sudden the only job we can get is the one you're offering."

"It sounds like you can all thank Tim for that. If I'm to be your singer then we need to have trust between us."

"Trust?" said Whistle all contemptuous.

"Singer?" said Belle, her leadership sensitivities piqued.

"Yes I will be your singer. It's all part of accepting this opportunity. Once you do so, things are going to change."

There was silence around the table as we tried to make out how we felt about our situation. Had we been saved or damned? And why was it so difficult to tell the difference? I think at this point it came down to general outlook on life. Those of a naturally hopeful outlook plumped for aspects of the situation suggesting we might be saved. Long Tom, I could tell, had gone over to that positive side, helped there by a nice portion of game pie. Belle was somewhere in the middle, still to make a judgement, while Whistle acted with the hauteur of a man kidnapped from the open highway and held against his will in a very nice restaurant.

"I don't like being deceived," growled Whistle.

"That's enough from you," snapped Belle, who amidst her

reflections, now seemed to have made an abrupt decision about which side of fate's bargain to align herself. "We have no employ and nowhere to live, which means we are without the luxury of any high horse. Alright Eddie, I am going to assume that you have our best interests at heart. So, you should stop messing about and explain your offer."

Eddie smiled his showman smile and threw back his long black hair, in that way of his which suggested that here was a new moment. It was his method of punctuation.

"This is work offered by people who wish to remain discreet. We are looking for a new type of music, so do not want established acts. I think you will be perfect. But be warned, once you enter our world it is unlikely you will want to go back to what you knew before. Still, from what you say, there isn't anything to go back to, is there?"

"No," confirmed Whistle who could be relied upon to be the first with bad news.

"If this is a job where I can do more drumming, then I'm in," confirmed Long Tom.

"Good," said Eddie.

"So this is definitely a show business proposition then?" queried Belle.

"Yes, of course it is. I said so before. You will be involved in musical performance, of a groundbreaking kind. We want the sort of music you are working on already, which means it won't be a stretch for you. Accept first and then I'll introduce you to our people. There is an event here at Rules tomorrow and I want you in attendance."

A crucial moment had arrived and as with most crucial moments, there were two things leaning on our decision. The first was the need to make a choice without having enough information to go on. The second was that despite appearances, our decision, in the end, was inevitable and dictated by circumstance.

"So, what's it to be?" asked Eddie.

"I already said what I think," declared Tom with some pride.

"Will there be money?" asked Belle.

"There'll be money, don't worry about that."

"And lodging?" challenged Whistle.

"Yes; and it will be a step up on your present arrangements. We have a house for you in Birdcage Walk."

"Birdcage Walk? We accept," confirmed Belle.

"Money, fancy lodging - why didn't we accept before?" marvelled Whistle.

"Well, we're accepting now," grumbled Belle.

My world had fallen apart to make way for a new one. A tide had gone out, and a new one had surged in, as fast as it does over estuary mud flats.

"Will we be going to our lodgings right away?" Whistle asked with some wideness of eyes.

"We can move over to the property which we are currently preparing."

"Preparing?" quizzed Belle. Maybe there was an echo of domestication in this professional girl, who would not be happy with half a house.

"It is far enough along to take you."

This seemed enough reassurance.

"How many bedrooms will there be?" asked Whistle. "Want to bunk with me, Belle?"

"Go bake your own head," was the reply.

It was not for the first time that I wondered as to the nature of Belle and Whistle's relationship. They did not seem to like each other overmuch. But I had seen many a husband and wife who disliked each other more than they, so arguing and bickering was no guide.

"You will each have a bed in your lodgings. We will go there shortly. And just a final warning and reminder that we are a secret organisation. At least until the time is right, you must not speak to others about our work. If you do, there will be trouble."

Once again I was not impressed by this talk of secrecy. Neither would you be if you knew the secretive habits of just about every trade guild in the East End. Tanners, candle makers, paint mixers, they all had their secret societies. It was no skin off my nose if learning the funny handshake of Eddie's self-important performers' society meant there was a roof over my head and food on my insides. I looked around at my fellow artistes. From their expressions they all appeared to be of the same mind.

"It's fine, Eddie," said Belle, with a contract confirming nod. "We will come and work for you."

And so it was, with London all gas lights and mystery, Eddie Mulsara led the way into Maiden Lane. Thanks to the services of a cloak room, he had completed his Regency rig with a flowing grey overcoat and a gold-topped rosewood cane, which in his hands served as fashionable accessory, aide to visual communication, and, I suspected, formidable weapon if the outlook required. He hailed a pair of hansom cabs - using the cane to amplify a request that brooked no objection. Once embarked, our motley crew headed up west, in the direction of St James's.

CHAPTER 8

We were to stay in a house on Birdcage Walk, overlooking St James's Park. The rooms had ceilings of a height that was ample for the flight of any caged bird. But I will tell you more about the house later, because on that first night, exhaustion did not allow me to register much, beyond grandeur and sparse furnishing. The following morning, we woke up late, whereupon after a brief period of sitting in the echoing front room, upon chairs that appeared to be abandoned rather than placed, Eddie rounded us up. He then took us on a return trip to Rules Restaurant for what he called early 'luncheon' which as far as I could make out was lunch, with a *shun* sound on the end for the sake of effect.

It was at Rules Restaurant where I found out exactly how my life had taken a trip down the river. Most of the time, routine stops you seeing things. But changes allow you to see through to strange brightness beneath the everyday. Everything presented itself to my eye in sharp relief. Each moment was new and took longer than usual to unfold.

As on the previous evening, I sensed something about the ambiguous nature of Rules, a place that accepted all kinds of sirs and madams. After listening to some chat amongst its clientele, I now came to understand the basis for this tolerant atmosphere. Rules was a place not for London's upper crust or lower echelons, but for show business coves, who are a manner of person you can never quite tie to high or low. They float in their own place, which is degraded far below the poorest orange seller and exalted in some moments above monarchs. Everyone here really was a sir, or madam. All you had to do was act your part. Long Tom was good at it. I watched him head off to the spread of food and start picking and choosing as though he did this sort of thing regularly.

"That quality looks like the Prince of Wales," I remarked to Eddie, nodding towards a red-faced, bearded, evening-suited gent engaging in hail-fellow-well-met carrying-ons in a far corner.

"That's because it is the Prince of Wales."

"What?"

"That can't be the Prince of Wales," scoffed Whistle.

"Lots of gents look like the Prince of Wales," said Belle. "It's the fashion."

"That gentleman set the fashion because he actually is the Prince of Wales," said Eddie, affecting the nonchalance of a man who often joins princes for luncheon.

"It does look like him," said Whistle turning his worried face to me. "I don't know what's going on, but I'm not sure I like it. You know what? I think we should leave. We might be able to start again in another town where they don't know us."

"There's someone you have to meet," declared Eddie, ignoring Whistle's wobbles.

Eddie led the way through a busy hubbub towards a young woman, who was an order of person I had only ever seen in periodicals. I have to say, until the moment I laid eyes upon this lady, there was an instinct that inclined me to agree with Whistle - maybe our fortunes would be better served by going somewhere foreign. Once I saw this girl, such thoughts were gone from my mind.

Atop coiled, dark hair, a straw hat gave the strong suggestion of rowing regatta.

Belle was casting me a look askance.

"Think she's a fine lady, Tim?"

When I failed to answer, Whistle gave his opinion.

"She is the jammiest bit of jam."

I have no idea what Long Tom thought, continuing with his earnest work at the food table.

So, back to the young lady. She had the sort of lovely, compact face, which looks more natural and beautiful when carrying a serious expression. Below her elegant confederation of facial features, there was a white shirt, somewhat frilly at the front, with a high collar and a neck scarf, done up like a rose. Layered over this came a jacket, the colour of cucumber ice cream, with upper arms all decorative folds of fabric, while the forearms came down close about the wrist as if ready for work. The britches were similar, initially silly pleats, but only to the knee. Heading down to a shapely ankle, all was close fitting and sensible, as were a pair of black, flat shoes.

"I'd like to meet her tailor," remarked Belle.

Eddie was about to introduce us, when who of all people should walk in but Smalt. After cringing his great height through the Rules doors, he blenched his way across the restaurant, carrying something, longer than it was wide, fatter at one end than the other. This odd object resolved itself into something that looked like a musical instrument that had melted, its outlines blurred into lumpen indistinctness.

I had no desire that Smalt see me, as it was not clear if Blackwell had yet been paid. In the event, hiding behind Eddie was unnecessary. Smalt shot a brief glance of recognition; but it was a humbling gander that suggested I was a messenger and writer of navy particulars, not a man of import. Either the money problem was proceeding down other channels, or more likely Blackwell had been paid and Old Ma was trying to manage the loss.

Without ceremony, the lovely lady in the straw hat pushed

a few plates aside upon a long table.

"Please put the item here," she said in a voice that was a little odd around the edges.

She thus directed Smalt to place his cargo in the cleared space. Then she set to popping open a curving line of chrome fasteners in what I now decided might be an encasement for some kind of musical instrument lying within. Smalt helped pull back the leather flap to reveal something bearing resemblance to a Spanish guitar. But the Spanish guitar was an ancestor, like a dinosaur bird made of string and leather lay in the ancestry of an eagle.

The lady liberated this strange guitar from its case, as though she were lifting an infant from a cradle. Her critical inspection appeared to reduce Smalt to a state where he might at any moment faint upon the glittering, though disrupted, Rules table. His mood improved when it became clear that the outcome of this inspection was satisfactory, communicated by a warm smile and clumsy patting of Smalt's shoulder, clumsy because that mighty shoulder was too far from the ground to easily reach.

After said patting was complete, the lady started fussing with cables, running from the guitar to something unseen through a swinging restaurant door. Smalt lumbered to those same doors, leaning through to shout to someone unseen:

"Ready to raise steam, master."

During this hiatus in proceedings, I demanded answers.

"Eddie, just what is going on here? What have we got into?"

"You have just met Maisie Gladwish."

"She is very modish," commented Belle.

"Could we be introduced?" asked Whistle with suavity that was not becoming.

"Oh, please," was Belle's exasperation. "Maisie looks like a woman of big parts, and you are a small man."

"So, what is it that she does?" I asked Eddie, trying to remain factual.

"You could say she's an inventor."

Maisie came back towards us, running a cable along the floor beside my feet. This was an opportunity and I took it.

"How do you do?"

Maisie continued to focus on the cable, following it onwards to the kitchen doors.

"Never mind, sweetie," was Belle's comforting remark, thinking I had been snubbed.

"A young lady's dream, you are," mocked Whistle.

"She's deaf," said Eddie.

"Deaf to your charms," smirked Whistle.

"She's deaf," repeated Eddie, "to Tim's charms, and to sounds."

Belle looked concerned.

"You mean she can't hear? But how can that be? She was talking to Smalt."

"I know she was talking, but she is deaf, and has been since she was about twelve years old. Totally deaf in the left ear, with a very slight hearing on the right. That's where all this began. You see, she worked with a man called Alexander Graham Bell, both a teacher of the deaf, and an inventor."

Eddie sat at the somewhat disarranged table. Us confused band of musicians sat down beside him, even Long Tom, whose attention had been dragged away from the food.

"So when you say Alexander Graham Bell," queried Belle, "do you mean that cove who invented telephones?"

"The very same. He didn't just invent telephones. As I say, he is also a famous teacher of deaf children."

"A teacher you say?" said Whistle. "Is that just an amusing

fact?"

"No. That is the key to what I'm trying to tell you. After showing early genius in mathematics and design, Maisie's parents wanted the best education for their daughter. They certainly had the means to provide it. The family owns a big house near Hyde Park, and other places too. As Maisie became deaf following a bout of scarlet fever, they determined that they would find the best of teachers, settling on Alexander Graham Bell in America. As it turned out, this was not a successful enterprise. Despite good intentions, Alexander Graham Bell couldn't help but think of deaf people as deficient. Maisie did not take kindly to this. Then, instead of showing her feelings, she asked to look at the great man's laboratory. Assuming deafness necessarily implied lack of intellect, a technician provided a tour. It was perfect cover. The witless guide made no effort to hide what amounted to valuable commercial secrets. Maisie took it all in, storing everything in her photographic memory. Did you know that Thomas Edison is deaf? Well he is. Edison says that deafness serves to aid concentration. Anyhow, stored in her head, she brought all of Graham Bell's work back with her to London. With her parent's support, she set up a workshop. She took ideas, mere concepts that could not yet work, and set to turning them into reality."

Eddie screwed up his showman's face as he tried to concentrate on the mechanical details that followed. He twisted the knife sideways on a spotless cotton tablecloth as a way of expressing confusion with technicalities.

"It's something about electrical currents that corresponded to sound waves. You can make electrical currents into sounds, which are then broadcast out by an amplifying sound box. Maisie set about making the sound box. As she'd enjoyed music since early childhood, she designed electrically powered instruments to drive music through her new devices, allowing her to both sense music with the little hearing she has left, as well as feeling it through vibration."

Explanation completed, the knife went back to its upright position.

"So are her parents here somewhere?" asked Belle, interested in the human element.

"Her parents died last year, out in India. It was a dreadful shock, but Maisie has carried on her work, under the patronage of Prince Edward. Her parents were friends of his."

Eddie interrupted his explanation, jumped to his feet, before heading through to the Rules' kitchen, where black magic seemed to be occurring. In the interval, Whistle inclined sideways towards Belle and me, his features heavy with conspiracy.

"Good friends, eh?" he leered. "I've heard about these royals. I would wager the Prince was better friends with the wife rather than the husband; and the husband wasn't too bothered. That's why His Highness is looking out for this young lady."

"You got your mind from Thomas Crapper himself," hissed Belle.

I reflected on all the complex hints that had just come out in Eddie's story of Maisie's background. I had no idea if Whistle's theory was true, but we were aware through Forbes that Prince Edward was definitely one for the ladies. Backstairs, he was known as Edward the Caresser.

Here's an observation you can have for free - an easy going approach to the matter of public morals is something you find in the highest and lowest of places. It's the middle that's the strict place. None of us were middling. As previously explained, here at Rules there was this feeling that we had entered a show business world where things are at their own level, which certainly wasn't in the middle.

I was just pondering on implications when Eddie returned with Maisie, her demeanour suggesting she had been pulled away from something important. She was carrying the guitar machine, with a cable dangling from its wider end.

"Here they are," said Eddie waving in our direction.

Maisie studied us.

"So, you are the kroomen musicians. You don't look like kroomen."

"No, we don't," confirmed Belle, in a woman-to-woman tone. "But we love the music, and think others will too, given half a chance."

"So introduce me."

"I'm Belle. I play guitar and sing. This is Whistle, who does likewise. This is Tom - drums."

"And the scrawny fellow?"

"That's Tim. He writes our words."

"So, Tim, what is it like writing words for this kind of music?"

"It's, you know, tricky. You have to let the beat, in a way, suggest, as it were, words, that spring unbidden, rather than the other way round to the way you would usually do."

I was nervous and mumbling, not keeping contact with Maisie's intense green eyes. I glanced up to see those eyes had narrowed.

"Mean what you say, say what you mean, Tim. I am deaf, and if you mumble, I won't be able to understand. And if you mumble, maybe you are not saying anything that I need to understand."

"Yes, quite, get your drift."

I looked at the red carpet.

"What's it like working with these boys?" This question was addressed to Belle.

"They're good boys mostly. Tim does not show competence with words just at this moment, but don't be deceived."

Trying to make up ground with Maisie, I decided on a second attempt.

"You talk so well, for, well, for someone who can't hear... I mean, I knew a cove in Rosemary Lane who had no hearing and no, eh, speech either. So... you speak well."

Why couldn't I just shut up?

"God save us," I heard Whistle mutter behind me. Maisie threw me another of her narrow glares.

"Yes, I can talk."

"Tim means no harm," commented Belle.

I smiled in what was meant to be a winning way.

Maisie picked up the musical instrument, resting the shiny contour of its body on her bloomer clad knee. It appeared that people out beyond the swinging doors were happy with preparations. An engineer in a flat black cap, who appeared to have jumped off the footplate of a London to Glasgow express, leant through and gave a jaunty thumbs up.

Maisie slipped off her shoes, so that her bare feet rested on the carpet, red with swirling gold foliage. Eddie noticed our curiosity at this bare-footed stance.

"It helps her feel the sound."

Thus divested of shoes, Maisie took a breath, closed her eyes, and swept her right hand across taut, metal strings, while the fingers of her left hand made a complex pattern on a long, fretted neck. A shower of sound sparks scattered into the air from a black packing case with a mesh front, set next to the kitchen doors. Maisie opened her eyes and strummed a more confident, second chord, bursting now like an eruption of lava, with embers flying into the upper reaches, while dark masses of scarlet, molten rock smouldered below.

"As I live and breathe," exclaimed Whistle.

"Now, it's your turn."

Whistle stepped forward his eyes aglow, seemingly reflecting the fire of those chords.

Maisie bypassed Whistle's approach, handing the guitar to Belle, who took it as a woman would take a baby from another woman.

"It's not too heavy, and it will balance in your arms."

After a kind of baby-bouncing settling in, Belle placed her left hand into fancy filigree on the fret board, before sweeping her right across strings seemingly purloined from a piano's insides. Another plume of sound lava burst from the creator, high-flying scintillations scattering above roaring masses of lower outpourings. Belle turned shining eyes upon us.

"Boys," she said, "I think we are going to have fun."

CHAPTER 9

The word destination has destiny in it. Perhaps it makes people more secure to know that the name for the place they are going has within it a purpose and a plan. The destiny in destination might take your mind off those unknown challenges that lie ahead. This was how I felt, exiled from home, throwing in my lot with musicians and inventors, charged with creating a style of electrical music which did not yet exist, all whilst pursuing a fearsome young lady who had turned my head.

Leaving Rules, I became separated from my musical comrades, which seemed like an accident but wasn't. Chasing down the Strand, I caught up with Maisie in Trafalgar Square. She appeared to be making for the Mall.

People walked in their throngs about Trafalgar Square. Some of them seemed to be heading off somewhere important. Others displayed a more casual sightseeing aspect. It made for a messy crowd, some parts surging, others wandering and standing. All about were pigeons, who one moment would be strutting in odd triangles, only for a signal from some pigeon admiral to send them rushing into the air, before coming down pretty much where they took off, before all the fuss and flying took place. Then they would be hopping again, with the corner of an eye alert for some crumb.

"I say," I called. "Hello."

Of course, she couldn't hear me. A tap on the shoulder didn't seem proper. Wheel in front of her perhaps, and give the music hall 'ta-dah'?

Too much thinking and not enough attention to the business of walking. Tripping was inevitable, but at least the bemusement and surprise of passers-by brought the attention of my beloved to your narrator.

"Ah, the writer boy. Are you alright?"

"Yes, very well," were my brave words. Struggling back into a standing position, I remembered the need for clear diction and to look at Maisie whilst talking.

"I was going to offer to escort you."

"Really? It does not appear that I am the one in need of escorting."

"No. I get your meaning. Why are you walking alone?"

"Because I do some of my best thinking while walking alone. Other people can be a distraction."

"Yes, they must be. Nevertheless, are you headed towards Birdcage Walk by any chance? We have been given lodging at some grand rooms there. It is prime."

"What does prime mean? Is that slang for high quality?"

"That is correct. I apologise for the occasional slip into the argot of the street."

"You speak in an odd way."

"I am aware. My speech is a gallimaufry of my background living amongst costers and finders, while pursuing an education at the feet of a disgraced Oxford don. So, what I meant to say is that I am on my way to our house in Birdcage Walk, which is very desirable."

I could hear the way I was talking, but somehow couldn't stop myself.

"I know where you're going. My people organised it for you. I am going there too, as it happens."

"Really?"

"Yes, but this walking is boring. Would you like to travel in a more exciting way?"

After meeting Maisie and hearing about her incredible technical accomplishments, I speculated on the wonders to which she might be referring.

"Are we to ride on an airship now?"

"An airship? No, you ridiculous boy. Come."

I fell into step beside Maisie, who looked at me with an amusement of shapely eyebrows.

"I have to ask, how did you manage to learn the guitar?"

Without thinking, I had asked this question whilst looking ahead. Determined fingers grabbed my chin and yanked us into eye contact.

"I won't say it again. Look at me when you're talking."

"Of course."

"And remember talking with me is better than talking to hearing people. You must be clear, and there can be no talking over each other. Taking turns is how it's done. If all communication were like that, imagine how much better things would be."

"Yes, I understand."

"Now, your lovely friend Belle said you are a nice lad really, so come with me and we will have an interesting journey to your house."

Maisie took me into a skein of alleyways near St James's Palace. Soldiers in bearskins did not salute as she passed, but neither did they jump to and arrest us, which was as good as a salute in my book. With this divine protection, we reached a small courtyard. To be walking unmolested in these surroundings gave proof that I really had fallen in with a secret society, rather than a glorified trade guild. Admittedly the shock of finding myself in this new situation caused my sense of proportion to temporarily leave its moorings. If this machine of transport we were seeking was not an airship, maybe it was a motorised carriage, which as well as delivering us to Birdcage Walk, might also have the power to travel into past or future. Maisie unlocked a door in a lean-to shed, revealing a brace of safety bicycles. I assumed that these apparently humble items could not be the object of our search. My curious eye roved for what we had really come for. But no, Maisie went over to the bicycles. Now her outfit made sense. She was wearing women's bicycle attire.

"We had these manufactured at Blackwell's for Prince Edward. They are amazing without being conspicuous, as your ridiculous airship would be."

I gave quiet thanks that I had made no mention out loud about machines for travelling through time.

At first glance these safety bicycles did not look too out-of-the-ordinary, until getting closer I realised there was something odd about the stack of cogs on the back wheel. These cogs ran from a large, tea plate affair at the lowest level, through gradations of cog size, to a small thruppeny bit at the top of the pile. There were also two extra cogs on a stalk beneath the central pile, giving the bicycle chain a rectangular appearance, rather than the usual elongated triangle.

"Come, I will show you how they work."

A brief instruction session followed in the yard where Maisie demonstrated the pushing of a little lever on the steering bars, which moved the bicycle chain amongst that stack of cogs. I did my best to concentrate on what Maisie was saying, about big cogs for hills and small cogs for flat. Some more basic lessons were required first, regarding the technique needed to balance on two wheels.

Let us simply say that when I rode out into the London evening behind Maisie, I'd already copped a few shiners. Nevertheless, in Maisie's opinion, a boy who claimed to be a writer must be clever enough to pick up the idea of bicycling in short order.

I don't know how I lived through those first ten minutes. Throwing myself into a new life beyond Blue Anchor Yard was as nothing compared to throwing myself out onto two wheels in pursuit of a young lady who was, in her own words, a competent velocipedestrienne. When you are trying to impress a velocipedestrienne, you do not admit that defying the natural laws of gravity is beyond you. You make your best effort to balance on a kind of spinning, mechanical tight rope.

Just so I could have more time to gain experience, Maisie doubled back towards Trafalgar Square, rather than heading directly for Birdcage Walk. Some of the pigeons didn't even have the decency to scatter at my collisions with the ground. They merely stepped to one side and continued pecking. Opening my eyes, I would see life from their level for a few seconds. The sour, sideways look in a pigeon's eye is clear when you plunge down into their world. Maisie failed to witness many of these calamities, being the sort of girl who looks ahead rather than behind. She knows my pain, I was thinking. She just thinks this is the best way to learn.

Cycling taught me many lessons between Trafalgar Square and St James's Park.

Answering my knock, Eddie opened the heavy door of our house in Birdcage Walk. He took a step back at the sight presented to him.

"My God, your tosher friends caught up with you, did they?"

"No, I'm in good health. I've just been learning how to ride a bicycle. Listen I've brought someone back with me."

Maisie who had been sorting out the bicycles, poked her head into view around the door frame.

"Eddie, darling."

"Maisie."

They embraced right there on the threshold. I felt in a bewildering sort of way as if I were still on two wheels.

CHAPTER 10

I had to jump to it and accept things that evening. First on my list was accepting the idea that Maisie and Eddie were especial friends. I had no idea where they had met and did not feel that I could ask.

The second thing it was necessary to become accustomed to was my new home. The big salons and bedrooms of our Birdcage Walk house were enough of an adjustment, though they were rather bare of furniture, which made me feel as though my mode of living was very smart bivouacking, rather than proper habitation. But the rooms I had seen so far were as nothing compared to the basement, where Maisie now led us. This chamber appeared to be a place just for rehearsing music. A number of Maisie's incredible guitars perched upright in stands designed for their curving contours. Off in one corner stood a grand piano, its slabs of black, lacquered wood reflecting an electrical glitter of Edison bulbs recessed in the ceiling.

"This is our studio for recording," declared Maisie.

To the left of the door as you came in, stretching most of the length of one wall, was a large window fronting an adjoining room beyond.

"What's going on over there?" asked Whistle nodding towards the odd window arrangement.

"We're still working on that," said Maisie. "It's called the control room. We will direct music recording from there. More information will be available in due time. For now all you need to know is that this is where we can make our new music. We placed the room below ground level to protect us from prying ears. The necessary electric power for our equipment comes from a steam driven turbine, set up in an out-building behind the house."

I tried to take in all this information, whilst Belle, dipping a white cloth into a bowl of water and astringent, bathed my cycling wounds.

"Our work is still classified," Eddie was saying, "but it's only preparation for the time when our secrets can be revealed. Maisie is too talented to hide away forever."

The dabbing of moist fabric upon skin became more ferocious, as the cloth encountered a patch of crusty blood on my upturned face.

"Belle, that's a little firm."

"Oh, don't be a baby."

I screwed up my willpower, in an effort to remain quiet. This allowed me to listen to what Whistle was saying.

"Alright, I see this is interesting. But I have to ask. Why bother with music? Maisie, you seem to be some kind of genius. Why don't you make airships, or machines for travelling through time?"

Eddie stared at Whistle, giving him enough time to reflect on what he just said, and regret it.

"Tsk, tsk," I mocked through my pain, conveniently forgetting that I had been talking about airships myself earlier.

"What is this obsession with airships?" snapped Maisie. "Forget them, and machines for voyaging beneath the sea, or for going backwards and forwards through time. And put out of your mind metal men driven by clockwork mechanism. Forget all that. Forget machines, because in the end what is the use of science without art? If the world has to be changed by science then so be it, but art will have to develop as well, to make something human out of the science. That is how we intend to bring an artistic revolution to run alongside an industrial one. We start right now, so Belle you'll just have to leave Tim as he is. You've tidied up the worst, and it's not as if we have him around for his looks."

Smalt helped Maisie trail cables to three guitars leaning in their stands. He picked up the first guitar and presented it to Belle, bowing as he did so. Whistle received the second in a rather more relaxed manner. The third guitar, Maisie picked up herself. This instrument had fewer and thicker strings.

"I will play an electrified guitar basso. I can feel the low notes more easily, so I will be providing a base line. And for Tom..."

Maisie nodded towards what looked like a jumble of crates covered with a sheet. Smalt obliged by pulling aside the covering, revealing a collection of drums, disposed in a layered semicircle, a kind of percussive Giant's Causeway, with a fat base drum tipped upon its side at the front. Golden, circular tea trays balanced themselves atop stands each side of the arrangement. I realised these must be cymbals.

Long Tom extended himself to his feet.

"Did you make these?" he asked Smalt.

"I assisted the master."

Smalt was the next to get a shock when Long Tom hugged him.

"Thank you, Smalt."

Arms that had once threatened to throw me into the Thames, hung in the air each side of our emotional drummer.

"I have no words..."

"Tom," chivvied Belle when the hug continued. "Let Smalt go. Just try your new drums."

Releasing our embarrassed technician, Tom appeared to have forgotten about the necessity of breathing. There was a certain shame for me in seeing that even in his state of excitement, Tom still had the presence of mind to turn and face Maisie when he spoke to her. And because he was a man of few words, the words he did say were expressive and to the point.

"This truly takes the egg."

Tom settled himself amongst his tumble of percussion.

"There's some drumsticks on the floor there," said Smalt, now standing well back, seemingly fearful of another emotional display.

"Thank you, but I will use my own."

These personal sticks rarely left Tom's person.

"You play the base drum with a foot pedal. Do you see?" said Smalt pointing from his safe distance.

Why waste words when Tom could send three, deep thumps across the room. There followed a torrent of concussions, punctuated with thrilling golden tea-tray crashes. Tom shot out a hand and stilled the tea-tray ringing.

"Thank you," is all he said.

So, we sat down to create a new kind of music.

A few hours later, no one was feeling happy and excited. Even the presence of a genius did not make writing a song easy. And I'm not talking about myself, obviously. I'm speaking of Maisie, whose brilliance did not extend in a poetic direction, which is why she looked with impatience to me. I don't know if you have ever tried to write a song, but it is very, very hard. Imagine trying to make up not just a new song, but an entire new style of lyric writing, with determined artistes pressuring you, all just after losing your home. You will then begin to appreciate the difficulties. It was fortunate that we had already made some headway during rehearsals in the Wilton cellar. That is why Eddie had picked us, because we were part way along the path that he and Maisie envisaged.

We started with the song we had been toying with at the

Wilton, about the music hall woman. Belle and Whistle had made more of their bendy riffs, which suited Maisie's electrical instruments just fine. And Long Tom was circling effectively on his wonderful new drums. But then moving on from this familiar ground to a new work was slow going. Eddie appeared to believe that songs might spring into existence ready-made, like sheet music coming off a printing press. Attempting to make a song out of nothing is the most agonising thing, like trying to do a jigsaw, when the pieces are something you have to manufacture yourself before you can fit them together into a picture you can't yet see. Adding to my floaty feeling of confusion was this underground room, cut off from night and day. It could be anytime upstairs. Time fell into suspension beneath the endless illumination of Edison bulbs.

Eddie held the opinion that grog helped his creative process, though he wasn't doing much creating - that was me on the words, Belle and Whistle on the melody, with Tom and Maisie on the rhythms. I had a pile of sheets covered in lines scrubbed through, some crossed with enough vigour to break through the fabric of the paper. Taking this pile, I squared my sheets off and placed them upon the table. It was a gesture necessary to maintain control.

"Come on, Tim," moaned Eddie, soused and prowling. "Give us some words. Give us something, anything."

"So, Almanac says a few nice things about me, says I've read some books and written a few things and you think that all qualifies me to come up with a whole new type of lyric writing in half an hour."

"This is hard," said Maisie. "It's harder making music than designing the instruments to make it."

"This is impossible," clarified Eddie. "How do we do it? How? Tell me?"

It was no good squaring sheets of paper now, but I continued to do so. This enraged Eddie. Storming up to my table, he swept my neat pile onto the floor.

"Come on," yelled Eddie, "get on with it. What are you thinking about?"

"I'm thinking about your ridiculous, afternoonified clothes, if I'm honest. How can you be kroo looking like that? They would laugh at us."

Just before the disaster with muddled royals, back in my old life, Almanac had me reading poetry by Byron. Eddie's manner of dress was as I imagined Byron might have favoured when on duty as a romantic poet, his outfit all claret red, with white lace trimmings at the cuffs, his round-me-houses anchored by a wide, black belt and extravagant silver buckle.

Long Tom started banging out an insistent beat.

"Come on," he shouted.

"Let me think," I pleaded.

"Don't think, darlin'," suggested Belle.

"Yeah, he might be good at that," sniped Whistle.

"Even if we got something, how do we know if it's good or not?" I wailed. "This is all so new. There's nothing to go on."

Tom slackened his rhythm, and comforted himself with desultory ripples of percussion.

"We'll feel it," declared Belle. "And this music is not new really. We are building on a tradition that is very old."

Then with the guitar equivalent of bashing her hands down on the keys of a piano, she flung her hand across the strings before slumping herself and her instrument into a wing-backed chair. I picked up my scattered sheets of paper from the floor, more a discombobulated clerk than a songwriter.

And thus we sat, with only Tom's thoughtful tapping for company.

"Maybe this is madness," declared Whistle. "If you take a minute to think about it, this is complete madness."

Most days are shaped by the routine of things carrying on, like a machine to ease your travel through time. Maybe a machine for travelling through time does exist. It is our daily round, the routine that gets us up in the morning and puts us to bed at night - a kind of endless shanty that keeps everybody moving, so that suddenly ten years can get behind you. But sometimes routine is disrupted. Then there is a moment of loss, a moment of choice. Will you slip back to the old ways, which even in being hard and relentless, have their own easeful, workaday momentum? Or will you try for something new? The time of change is truly a wilderness. Routine years can go by more easily than a moment in that wasteland. We sat there now, marooned in the primeval darkness of night, lit by a glow of new electricity.

All was hopeless. We couldn't be kroo. A foppish young singer, a lady engineer, a lost writer, a duet who argued, and a drummer of few words - who were we to capture in electric music the spirit of kroo? Those men had to be heard to be believed. They didn't have to try to do what we were trying to do. It was their daily round. Anyone within earshot came for the ride. Listening to kroo was the only thing in the world that could make toting barrels for the Royal Navy into a worthwhile course of action.

We sat in that moment, trapped in time. A whole novel could pass there, pages, chapters, introductions and appendices. I fell into a kind of trance, not thinking back or forward.

"I'm going for a walk," said Eddie opening the door.

The door swung open, just at the moment when Big Ben sounded from across St James's Park. I heard the short, playful introductory tumbling of chimes. A pause followed this sequence, an empty gap waiting for a new hour to ring. That interval was the sound of us sitting between an old life's lost habit, and a new round which might take its place. Then, just when it seemed as though the silence would last forever,

Big Ben's first midnight chime burgeoned through the night, into our basement studio, the first outside intrusion we had experienced in hours. As the first chime dissolved, a second followed, taking up the slack of the first. Seemingly, for her own amusement, Belle started to play a slow, ominous riff across that distant and ponderous iron beat. This musical figure asked a question upwards, followed by a query downwards, coming to a conclusion that descended in three steps. Belle asked the question twice more. On the third repetition, Maisie picked up her guitar basso, stood with her stockinged feet resting firm on the floor and answered the question, taking the three steps down deeper yet by accompanying Belle's descending notes on her base. Eddie froze on the first few steps of the stairway.

It occurred to me that Big Ben sent out the right sort of beat for those aiming to bring music to a new, industrial world. A night-filling, mechanical sound reaching for miles, a sound you could feel - that was what we were to work with.

Long Tom started stroking beats onto the cymbals, getting three beats in the big spaces between Big Ben booms. Then he backed up the cymbals with deep beats on his foot operated base drum, before laying a driving top beat on his snares. Whistle joined in, asking the same questions as Belle, from a slightly higher point of view, before stepping down into the same conclusion. My skin started to prickle. There was an itch in my throat, which turned into words, carefully directed so that Maisie could see them.

"Thunder rolls, the world disjoints its frame...The night is dark with a soaking rain... lightning arcs across the skies... A new life starts, while the old one dies."

By now Maisie and Belle were rolling round their riffs, looking in amazement at each other, catching Whistle's eye, all his cynicism turned to wonder. Big Ben's final chimes were now faint and echo-like, sitting off the beat in the circling, musical phrase. Maisie leant back as if supported by the rumbling of her baseline. My pile of paper shook.

Eddie came back in and shut the door. This was the beginning.

CHAPTER 11

Back in Blue Anchor Yard there was no such thing as solitude. It was odd, the first time I found myself alone in the Birdcage Walk house. There was luxury in sitting by myself. To write I had taken a small room on the top floor, with sloping ceilings, smooth and white. A desk beneath the window looked over a view unrolling in stages, as if made by a painter who had given careful attention to perspective. The East End doesn't have any perspective, just a hurly burly right up against your eyes and soul. The only place for perspective is out on the river, where grey distance appears magnified through a tangle of masts, rigging and crane derricks.

My new view out of this window was something else. First, there were the tops of trees, which served to save our house from rough and ready proximity to traffic on Birdcage Walk. Then came the green expanse of St James's Park, the Mall's grand mansions beyond that, standing against lavender-crenellated cloud mansions hanging in a wide, pink evening sky. And all of this was doubled and inverted in the shining mirror of St James's Park Lake. It was beautiful and not a little distracting when you are busy trying to invent a new character of lyric.

I was alone, with no one to pull me up for my lack of concentration. In my old life I had longed for time like this, to get on with my work. Now that I had it, my thoughts were filled with Belle, Whistle, Tom, Eddie and Maisie, who were all out buying new togs with the benefit of their retainer, which was moderately generous. My solitude was not so luxurious after all. In fact, it became unpleasant. Is all luxury of this ambivalent nature? I was glad to hear my band mates approaching the front door. Discerning the faint sounds of argument, I rushed downstairs to see what was transpiring.

Throwing open the door, Maisie stalked into the living room, followed by a swaggering Eddie. There was much high dudgeon in these various gaits. Belle and Whistle followed across the threshold, with less dudgeon and rather more of the awkwardness that comes when other people are arguing while you are not. Long Tom was a rear guard, eating a portion of hot chestnuts from paper.

"Ah, it's darling Timmy," said Belle.

"Written anything?" asked Maisie.

"Working on a few ideas."

"Well forget that," grumbled Eddie. "We have a visitor coming. He wants to write a song with you."

"It'll be fine," reassured Belle. "Tim will make something of it. He wrote Bells of Hell, didn't he?"

"Have we steam in the boiler?" interrogated Maisie.

"Yes, it's been cooking nicely while you've been gone. Smalt has been keeping an eye."

"We haven't got time for this, Maisie," sulked Eddie, who turned to your confused narrator. "She didn't consult me of course, even though I'm the lead singer in this band."

"Lead singer?" I queried. "What's one of those?"

"He's making up words," said Belle to Maisie with womanly confederacy. "He's a lead singer."

"Normal words aren't good enough for his highness," remarked Maisie.

"Would you mind telling me who is coming?" I said in what aspired to be a firm tone.

"It's just Prince Edward," confirmed Long Tom between nut mouthfuls.

"We must look after him," commanded Maisie. "He is our chief patron."

Even though I had seen this alleged Prince Edward at Rules, I still found myself wondering if in reality, Prince Edward was a stage name for one of Eddie's friends. Back in Rosemary Lane we had a few people who called themselves prince this, that or the other. It suggested both a certain measure of personal power, tempered by depreciation, which guards against the jealousy that inevitably follows a successful coster concern. We have our aristocracy too, who protect their position in all kinds of clever ways. No need to worry about Prince Buster of the match sellers. He's special but still one of us. See how it works?

There was a knock at the door, formal in nature. I can't quite remember how the pattern of raps went. It was a combination of rhythm, volume and intent, which all combined to say that this door was an impertinence and will open whether those of us on this side liked it or not. Black Rod might as well have been wielding his stick at the House of Commons.

Maisie knew from our reactions that the knock had sounded. She strode forward, opening the door to reveal an elegant woman who did not look like the source of a knock such as I had just heard. But you can never tell with people.

"Maisie, how lovely to see you. And these must be your musician friends I have heard so much about." The woman crossed our threshold, before turning towards a large figure emerging from the shades behind her.

"His Royal Highness, the Prince of Wales," she announced.

In strode Prince Edward, the walls and ceiling scrunching inwards with some violence, so that even this grand establishment in Birdcage Walk felt like a playhouse. He wore a greatcoat, with fur-lined collar turned up to protect its wearer from the rain of a dark and stormy night, though it happened to be a cool evening and not stormy at all. Our visitor removed this covering garment. Beneath was a further jacket, flaring around him from a top button below a lilac cravat.

"Good evening," said our visitor carefully facing his host. "So nice to meet you. I hope you don't mind this intrusion?"

"Of course not, Your Highness," reassured Maisie.

Your Highness, correctly used. Everyone seemed to know about that except me.

"Come in," continued Maisie. "Let me take your coat. This is Isabelle Rafferty and William Thistle, who go by the name of Belle and Whistle in their stage work. And here we have Tom Harrison who plays percussion. Eddie Mulsara you already know of course."

"Eddie, my lad." A royal hand patted Eddie's back.

"And please, meet our wordsmith, Tim."

"Ah, Tim, the song writer." My hand disappeared in a royal grip. "You go by the one name do you? Like Byron, or Keats?"

"He's just Tim to us," said Belle scooting forward to interrupt. "That's his professional name."

Belle of course knew that my second name was Pysspott, and wished to spare the royal ears the name of my noble family.

The Prince cast a smile of benign warmth over our little household.

"Now, I want you to be careful, sir," said the woman. "For my own sake, your visits must be strictly limited to the timings I have found in the royal schedule. You must not deviate. It's a bit like Cinderella, the only difference being that we'll both be pumpkins if you are late getting back from the ball."

"I understand and appreciate the risk you are taking, Daisy. I will never forget it. Everyone, this is my old friend Daisy Brooke, a lady from whom I have learnt much and who has helped greatly behind the scenes."

Not quite knowing Daisy's position in the royal firmament, I wondered if she was to be addressed as miss, mrs or majesty. As at Rules, the usual gradations somehow no longer applied. She could be all of these things at the same time.

Edward turned to us.

"My official role is patron of course, someone keeping an eye on things in the background. But I'd be so grateful if, just for an hour, we could work on a song together."

"Are you like, the actual Prince of Wales?" I blurted.

"Indeed I am. But don't let that impress you. Someone in my position has very little power to command anything at all. Not only do I have negligible influence over matters of state, the simplest of freedoms - to go for a walk around the city when whim strikes, for example - are closed to me. I certainly cannot command a collection of words to form themselves into a song. You are all monarchs compared to me. This isn't self-pity. I know I am fortunate in material ways, but despite the best clergymen our Church of England can provide, there is something of a hole in my life. Please let me experience just a small measure of freedom with you for a while. I have heard such exciting things. I would like to contribute more than money, patronage and protection. But this is not something I can command. I throw myself on your mercy."

"Since you put it like that..." muttered Eddie in Maisie's direction. An expression of suppressed annoyance flashed over her features. Of course, I knew she hated unclear speech. And I'm sure she did not appreciate the lack of business acumen demonstrated in a failure of respect towards an important sponsor.

"What Eddie means is that we will be delighted to have you in our musical collaboration."

"Band. We've decided to call it a band, as in a band of outlaws," chipped in Eddie, responding to Maisie's subtle chiding.

"Now, that is good," chortled Prince Edward, his features

glowing with delight. "Thank you so much. You are right to have your reservations. I promise not to cause any trouble."

We all headed down to the studio, where Smalt was already supervising necessary pipes and cables. Tom climbed up behind his drums, while the rest of the band picked up their guitars.

We ran through our song about the music hall woman, which at this point was more or less complete. By the end, Prince Edward was slapping his leg along with the beat, a look of exultation on his face, the imprint of hand impacts on smooth trouser textile.

"My, that was marvellous, really spirited and full of vim. And now, if I may be so bold, I have an idea for a song. Of course you might reject my trifle out of hand, you especially, Mr Tim, as the poet of the band."

"Come along, Your Highness," encouraged Belle, "Tim is good. He might be able to help."

Prince Edward paused, looked inward at who knows what royal childhood discomfort and loneliness, whereupon he not so much sang as spoke his words:

"One day I might be king, and tomorrow, you could be queen."

Then there was silence.

"That's all I've got so far."

"Well, it's a start," was my reaction.

Prince Edward lent forward, expectant.

"Yes..."

Making very sure Maisie could see my mouth, I embroidered some words about everyone waiting to become a king or a queen of their own kingdom.

"I wait for the king I will be later today, a monarch I will be each in our way. I wait for a queen who can finally say, the words of my speech in an Adelphi play. I wait to feel my memories stray, to when I strutted in the pomp and stomp of my day. There we will sit in a towering palace, bright as the light of aurora borealis. There we will be, as the people will pray, to the monarch they are and will never betray."

I hadn't had time to think, which in the perverse nature of these things meant that, on this occasion, the words came out quite easily.

Once I'd reached the end of my verse, Edward sat back in astonishment.

"That is remarkable. I have spent my life waiting to be king, and you take that experience and apply it generally. Is that what song writing is?"

"It might be."

I glanced at Belle, who was smiling in an affectionate manner in my direction, whilst also giving Maisie a sideways hug that spoke of pride in the way their little lad was turning out. I didn't know if that was quite the impression I was aiming to create with the girls.

There was no time to dwell on this, because Edward was busy trying to sing my words. His less than tuneful voice was gentle at first, getting progressively louder and more passionate. I had the impression that a few pre-performance drinks were helping in his rapid abandonment of strict, royal formality.

"Steady now," said Belle. "Let's get some music together for this one. Then we'll have Eddie try it out."

Long Tom started straight in, a circle of four beats on the cymbals - with the second beat of every four picked out on a snare, with a three and four thump on the foot-operated base drum. Whistle devised a sustained guitar line, which hung suspended, before falling away. Was that the sound of hope followed by disillusion, or of tension followed by relief? I liked the way it might be both. Belle came in with a chopping line that she started to play over the top. Then Eddie began to sing, the piece coming together quickly. There was some stop and start as we found our way, but after about half an hour we had a song that Eddie was building in intensity by stages. Edward looked on, his eyes shining with the joy of song writing, which was all the more joyful when someone else does the bulk of it for you.

I noticed Daisy Brooke consulting a pocket watch. It was clear that Prince Edward shouldn't really be here and that the rest of Britain's establishment would be unhappy if they knew that their cornerstone of tradition was involving himself in something so modish.

CHAPTER 12

For a month we would head down to the studio to continue our rehearsals, occasionally attended by Prince Edward when he could get away from his royal round. He contributed a few more words to our song about kings and queens, but mostly confined himself to happy observation.

It wasn't easy making this new music, or accepting the unfamiliar world that came with it. Even more confusingly, I now came to the realisation that new worlds have a way of circling around to head back from whence they came.

Let me explain.

During a rehearsal in the studio, Eddie, frustrated as usual that things were not progressing more quickly, grabbed one of Tom's drumsticks and began beating out a rhythm with it on one of the snares.

"Hey," objected Long Tom.

"Come on. Get some words to this rhythm."

It wasn't a complicated beat. It was just some whacking of a drum in frustration. It seemed unlikely that anything musical could come out of it, which underestimated the professionalism of my friends. After a few moments, Belle matched the concussions with chords that by turns sat together comfortably, and then grated against each other, like some new fashion, which looks ridiculous, then looks good, then looks ridiculous again. Whistle picked out an embroidery of notes above the basic melody. Maisie started to tack a base line, going up and down in alternating groups of slow three and quick six.

Eddie, apparently satisfied that he had started something, handed over the drum stick to its natural owner, whereupon Tom took up the work, turning a basically simple bounce into an enigmatically hypnotic meter.

I started to scribble some words about our angry singer's fancy clothes, just then in my eye-line. I weaved them round and about the subject of some young dandy flitting from one fashion to another, but doing so with wholehearted, abiding devotion. Fashions are flighty but they impose strict impositions. You have to be brave to go against their dictates.

Eddie saw I was now writing.

"Come on, come on," he was yelling.

I thrust a verse into his hands. Swaggering and easy, leaning into Tom's measures, he began singing about my devotee of fashion, who works so hard on ephemera.

I followed him down Burlington Row

Dressed in fashion from top hat to toe

The crease of his knapp, the press of his fold

It looks so new and so suddenly old

Stepping it out in leather and hose

Where fripperies lead that's where he goes

A journey that travels in cotton and linen

Always ending and always beginning

Circling round to that thing that he chose

It was one of these but is now one of those

The pace of his journey is rapidly spinning

Yet another ending and another beginning

The movement becomes a kind of repose

No so much walking as holding a pose

Eddie looked over at me in an expectant manner.

"I haven't got the rest yet."

"Dammit."

It took me a few hours to finish the whole thing, after which I sat back in my chair, listening to the band polishing and shaping.

And in the old world this would be the point where my chapter ends, because our song was done. But, dear reader, I tell you in all honesty, a new world is coming. I have to continue, because the song we had just finished could not be described as over. As I suggested at the beginning of this chapter, my new world had a compensating ability to bring back things that had once been.

This is how it happened. We sat behind the wide, glass window, fronting what Maisie was calling the control room, closed to us until today. I'd assumed it contained gear so new and dangerous that a window was needed to keep an eye on it. Not very technically minded, I admit to not giving the matter much thought. But then at Maisie's direction, it was to the control room that we retired following our rehearsal.

We entered a place that reminded me of a signal box above a busy junction on the Great Western. A table of switches and levers sat below the window, at which Smalt presided with not a little nervous self-sufficiency.

"What's this all about?" asked Whistle with his customary suspicion.

"This," said Maisie, "is where we control the machinery we are developing to capture our music. And that machinery begins with new microphones, which you can now see on stands around the studio."

I'd already noticed that Smalt had been in early, arranging a selection of poles topped with a strange globular structure fronted with a tight mesh grill.

"These microphones," continued Maisie, "are based on a David Edward Hughes design. Our version is much more advanced, better than anything from Edison or Berliner. The microphones pick up sound waves, which we then store on magnetic tape." With a blithe wave, Maisie indicated a tall cabinet behind us, where two hollow wheels ran in tandem, rusty-brown tape spooling between them. "Then it's a matter of transforming the magnetic patterns back into sound again with a separate piece of equipment." Another gesture indicated two packing-case sized boxes mounted on stands each side of the long window. Each box contained two dark concavities, a small one at the top, a larger below.

Eddie was standing beside Maisie grinning at us, amused I think by the expressions on our faces.

"Store the sounds?" This was Belle. She glanced at her partner. "Like one of those piano rolls?"

"Piano rolls? This is much more sophisticated," continued Maisie. "It's not just a piano we're talking about here, but all the instruments and voices that sit in front of the microphone. It will capture sound from all of them, turn it into a pattern stored in the form of magnetic particles. Smalt, if you would be so kind as to run the tape."

Then, not a word of a lie, Smalt turned to his control table, pushed sideways on a lever switch, which caused our music to sound in the air, emerging from those two packing cases, arranged each side of the window. Maisie might have poked fun about machines for travelling through time, but that's what she seemed to have devised. We had gone back to the music we made ten minutes before. Whether it was ten minutes ago, or twenty years ago today, it didn't matter, because this time machine brought it right back to our present moment. Never mind about the whips and scorns of time, they whipped and scorned no longer. Our music had reappeared from that undiscovered country from whose bourn no traveller returns. I had never followed Balzac's example of sticking my head in a barrel of rotten apples and taking a deep breath, but maybe the resulting state of mind felt like this. It was as though just for a moment barriers fell down, and the people who could attend a concert were not the ones who were actually within this room. Our audience could be anywhere and any when. Even you, dear reader, whenever and wherever you may be, could be here with us, listening to the band play. Welcome is all I can say.

Whistle glanced around, as though surrounded by a flock of invisible birds.

"What is this?"

"Pull yourself together, Whistle," said Eddie. "Is it so hard to understand? Our music has come back to play again."

"But this is even worse than piano rolls. We won't be needed anymore."

"We will. We could play in London, but people who can't travel to London will buy our recording and listen to us in Liverpool or Glasgow, or Paris. Don't you see what that means? One group of musicians could be getting proceeds from towns and cities the world over on the same night."

My ethereal moment of timelessness, dissolved into Whistle's practical business quibbles. I was back in the present moment.

"But I can't see people having all this gear in their houses," continued Whistle in a doubting vein, his gaze switching from noise boxes to tape spooler cabinet, to Smalt's desk of switches and levers.

"They won't need all this paraphernalia," said Eddie.

He walked to a table, located on one side of the control room. Here rested a wooden box, about the size of a large biscuit tin. We all proceeded to gather around this item. Eddie lifted a hinged lid to reveal a wheel within, like a potter's wheel, beside which stood a delicate, moveable arm with an appendage, reminding me of a domino, at one end.

"This is a machine for playing recording discs," announced Maisie.

"What recording discs?" asked Whistle.

"One of these," said Eddie. He had slipped away while our attention had been distracted. In his hand now lay a flat, square, card sleeve, of similar dimensions to the potter's wheel device. He tipped the card sideways, towards an open edge, whence emerged a black disc of a most remarkable aspect. The inner portion carried a circular paper label, as yet blank, which I assumed would carry an identification of the recording. Beyond that spread serried lines of minute grooves, catching the light in such a way that two parallel cones of efflorescence widened from the centre outwards.

"This is the recording in the form we will sell it for home use," explained Maisie, taking the disc from Eddie and holding it with her palms to its edges. "Sounds are faithfully stored in the form of tiny grooves. A needle, carried on the movable arm of the playing machine, travels in the grooves and renders potential sound actual. We are calling the disc a record, and our machine to reproduce the sound, a record player. Each record is a concert, available for anyone to buy and play as they will."

Whistle's eyes darted left and right. Was he trying to work out the financial arithmetic of all the potential 'concerts' which this disc would allow? Or did his befuddlement have a wider perspective, which involved not only muddles of money, but confusions of time and space so overwhelming that holding to questions of money helped him stay on an even keel? I glanced at Belle and I knew she felt it. There was a look we shared. She used no words. Maybe she could not speak of it. Words like to organise things, split them up into sentences and paragraphs. What we were experiencing was somehow the opposite of such orderly business. It was more like dipping in and out of Balzac's apple barrel. I will never forget that first time the barrier broke down between near and far, between a long time coming and a long time gone.

The music played on.

"I think we need to have the drums louder here," mused Long Tom, once again having the presence of mind to turn towards Maisie.

"And that's something else I need to explain to you," she replied. "We are not simply recording the sound onto one tape. This tape has up to six separate areas we can record onto. Smalt will be able to demonstrate. Just bring up Tom's drums, will you."

Smalt turned to his control table. With the movement of a slider on his control table, Tom's drums became louder so as to dominate the ensemble.

Not only could we go back to the past, we could tweak, see different aspects of it. We could erase parts we were embarrassed about. So you see, dear reader, why I did not end my chapter back at the conclusion of our rehearsal. In this new world, a final moment is not the end, since ends and beginnings are not what they were. The future must be a confusing place, open to perfection and great dissimulation. I felt a shift, more in my stomach than my head, sensing how exciting and disorientating life might be in the world to come.

CHAPTER 13

It is a tribute to the human power of adaption that not too long after those first nights, when the bells of hell rang out over wildernesses that lie between one life and another, I began to find a new kind of daily round. Writing, rehearsing, writing again. It was enjoyable and felt enough like a routine to give a sense that it might continue forever.

But of course, since this was a time of change, it wasn't long before something came along to bring disruption. A Post Office messenger arrived with a telegram from the paymasters and administrators of this operation, informing Eddie and Maisie that they were obliged to attend a meeting. They were often called in, to get updates on progress, or to receive pleas not to spend too much money due to the difficulty of hiding expenses in Crown Estate accounts. Through the window in front of my desk, I saw the pair making a hurried return from St James's. Eddie was not a natural hurrier, and neither was Maisie. Evidence of compatibility? I don't think so. The relaxed nature of a tardy person requires a punctual person like me to make the most of their qualities. I had this worked out. It was all about playing romance as the long game.

Eddie and Maisie made their entrance, always a sweeping affair of jackets and scarves.

"Now we don't want you worrying, Timmy." said Maisie.

"What's the matter," chimed up Belle with concern, from one of the armchairs, established in the living room for our leisure hours - of which there were not many. "Why should Timmy be worrying? It's not good for him to worry. He's sensitive."

"Belle, I'm not sensitive."

"Well, yes you are," confirmed Whistle, who had a large glass of wine, paid for by the Crown. He was drinking too much. For a man with the vulnerability, there is always an especial risk when someone else covers the cost of imbibing.

"I'm a writer, and excuse me but we have to be tough to cope with rejections. Anyway, please tell me, why should I be worried? I have been thrown out of my home and am now living in Birdcage Walk, crafting lyrics to African beat music. It all looks like a good, steady long term career to me."

This was a jest. As I have just recounted, my life was now more settled.

"The thing is," drawled Eddie, "word on the street has it that the toshers are after you."

"Word on the street? What does that mean?"

Eddie glanced at Maisie, offering her the chance to explain.

"Smalt says your people are looking for you," she said.

"Smalt says... he won't say anything about where I am, will he?"

By now, looking at Maisie when speaking was second nature, managed even in times of stress.

"Of course not," reassured Maisie. "He is our man and won't say anything. Nevertheless it would be best if you left London for a while."

"We were planning to head out of town anyway," said Eddie, "to stage a concert where we can try our music away from London. We can combine saving your neck with finding a venue. It will be an efficient use of time."

"Oh well, thanks very much. But the costers know all the

horse dealers and hansom cab drivers. They have links to traders at every train station. How am I going to get out of London without them knowing?"

"We have a plan," said Maisie, pointing through a window of Georgian proportions into the garden, cared for by hidden hands arranged by Prince Edward. It was odd being in this band. Everything was done for you. This was luxurious, but created a distance from practical concerns, which eventually might be damaging to the moral sense. Anyhow, that's a side issue. Back to the pressing matter of Old Ma setting her dogs on me.

Maisie's gesture carried my eye towards two bicycles propped up against the potting shed.

"How would you like to come on a bike tour with me?"

"Ohh," I said, "that would be lovely."

"You enjoyed your ride from Trafalgar Square."

"Indeed I did. Very exhilarating."

"You did fall off a few times."

"Oh, that was just because of careless items left in the thoroughfare."

Eddie flopped into an armchair and put a jaunty outside ankle up on opposite knee. His velvet and lace hung about him. He looked at Maisie.

"You really think this is a good idea, Maze?"

"No one will be expecting him to be on a bicycle. We have to look after our little lad."

"Yes, he is a bit vulnerable, I grant you that."

"Vulnerable? You come with me down a sewer, Eddie. We'll see who's vulnerable."

"But people aren't going to be wandering around sewers in a freelance capacity for much longer. Those days are over. Maze and me will look after you in your new life. And it's probably because the toshers are having such a tough time, that they are feeling extra sore about you losing all that reward money with your Victoria disaster. Maze thinks she can get you safely out of London on a bicycle. She rides all the time with her girls touring club. You will be an honorary member."

"I see."

"You'll be off at dawn tomorrow. Go to bed early. You'll need your strength."

"I don't think this is a good plan," contributed Belle, who, after all, was the one who bathed my wounds the last time.

"If Old Ma's men don't get him, the cycling will," remarked Whistle in his usual deflating way.

"Poor kid," was the only wisdom that Long Tom would allow.

CHAPTER 14

I was not at my best the following morning, wobbling over Westminster Bridge, dressed as a member of Maisie's cycle club for ladies. Before departure, Eddie had said that my delicate features made the disguise believable, which was disappointing at the time he said it, but reassuring when I came to suspect that hansom drivers looked especially vigilant this morning. My imagination tried to weave protective fantasies, rendering London as such a big and busy place, that it was unlikely a hansom cab driver's mind would focus itself on little me, now reduced to shaky cycling in a borrowed woman's bonnet and pale peach riding jacket. Then again, those drivers did look open-eyed, which is a difficult thing to achieve at an early hour, after travelling the same routes a thousand times. Was something different today? Was that difference me?

It's an odd thing that when you want people to take notice of you, following for example the publication of a book for whom you desire readers, no one pays you any mind. You're in a big empty room, shouting: 'does anyone want to read my book?' And the only reply is 'shut yer bone box,' heard from a distance. But when escaping attention is the aim, as on the occasion of having lost Old Ma a lot of gold and you're trying to get out of London on a bicycle you can barely ride, dressed as a swank young woman, then it seems as though eyes are looking at you from everywhere.

We crossed Westminster Bridge, and started to make our easterly way along the Thames. Maisie had a route planned out. We followed the river to Bermondsey, which is not a place for a fine young lady on a bike. Maisie acted as if she had every right to be a girl riding through Bermondsey. Her actions said 'look at me if you want to, I don't care', with the result that people failed to pay her much mind, which was more proof of that law of attention I was just telling you about.

It was necessary to strain every nerve to stay upright and change gears in the right way. But there was one compensation for having to try so hard to simply survive on two wheels. Such was the level of concentration necessary, we had reached Gravesend before I really knew what was going on. Here Maisie said I could discard my disguise, which was a relief, because the headgear was not, in my opinion, designed for vigorous exercise. It caused chafing from above, to add to that coming from below.

If you were running for your life from vengeful toshers, wouldn't you have thought that a disguise, once it has out-lived its usefulness, could be tossed in a hedge? Not Maisie. She had this bit arranged as closely as everything else about the trip. Gravesend, well out along the estuary, has the feel of a seaside town, with streets sloping down sideways to a promenade where the Thames masquerades as a half-mile wide ocean. It was at the front door of a house above this miniature briny deep that I stood aside as Maisie engaged in hugs and kisses with one of her girlfriends. This young lady had a hat-box full of protective pink tissue paper, all ready to enfold my disguise. It was necessary to apologise for a sweat stain on the bonnet's rim area. Fortunately this friend turned out to be a good hearted, outdoors sort of girl who said reassuring things about the power of bicarbonate of soda. She spoke with her hands to Maisie, who translated for me.

There were more kisses, even one for me. We then headed down hill to the promenade. Here Maisie indicated we should stop, directing me to lean my bicycle with hers against the promenade wall. With this achieved, she proceeded to unpack two neat satchels, which by some cunning means were suspended from a metal frame each side of the back wheel of her own bicycle. From these satchels appeared a tartan rug and a selection of greaseproof paper packages. Maisie announced that we were to have a picnic, which is an outdoor meal, taken upon a blanket. If this was running for my life, then it was fine with me.

And of course the main benefit of our escape attempt was the fact that I finally had Maisie to myself. I always called her by her proper name, rather than Maze, to distinguish myself from Eddie who acted like they had already been married these five years; or maybe, more accurately, had been brother and sister all their lives. I was respectful and courteous, feeling reassured that this strategy would win out in the end.

I plotted as we ate our picnic, watching ocean-going ships moving up river towards the docks near Blue Anchor Yard. Though they took my heart with them as part of their manifest, I tried to concentrate on the charms of my new life, most of which sat on the other side of this checkered rug, offering me chutney to go with cooked ham and bread. Maisie lent over to glance at some bruises resulting from tumbles I had taken. I was sure she would have bathed my wounds as Belle had done, but we didn't have the necessary materials to hand. Besides, the cursory nature of Maisie's inspection was probably a reflection of her thoughtful attempt to deflect any undue worry about minor scrapes.

The time came to saddle up again. Before we did so, it was necessary to swoosh away a group of onlookers who had gathered to stare at that odd arrangement of cogs on the back wheels of our bicycles. Tall black hats threatened to tumble off curious heads leaning down to take a closer look. I knew how to get rid of these people.

"It's a French thing," I said. "Parisian. It makes riding easier."

There was huffing and puffing.

"Must be a device to help the ladies," grumbled one Britisher.

"And small men," added his Britisher friend.

"It's effectively cheating," declared a third.

Satisfied with their dismissal of an effete, continental innovation, they wandered off to find something more British.

We cycled on down the Gravesend promenade, darted through some alleyways behind warehouses and then found ourselves out in wilds, the wildness of which I never thought could exist near London. It was as if the Thames had recently receded and we were riding along the one dry path that remained in this great expanse of former riverbed. The birds seemed to love it. They spent much ingenuity hiding themselves in reed banks and clumps of bushes, before ruining it all with a massed chorus of chirruping. At least in my flight from the vengeful toshers of Blue Anchor Yard I kept myself quiet, unlike these foolish birds. This was an odd trip, an escape with the feeling of a sightseeing tour. Maybe one day, people will travel about just for fun, and not have to be goaded into it by people who want to toss you in the river. Thinking about this, I found myself toying with lyrics for a new song...

Creepy monsters, scary shadow, running to a peaceful chateau

Driven onward by foes or friends, running headlong across hills and fens,

From highway robbers without a heart, from footpads whose pity starts,

Like a bank whose interest lends, in city streets where forgiveness ends

Then I fell off again, my rear wheel slipping sideways on a gravel canal path.

By the time we rode into the village of Upnor, I was

trying to do anything that might serve to distract from bodily discomfort. Focus on thoughts and not legs, I told myself. Live in the mind and not the body, because the body seems unable to sustain life much longer. Though my physiognomy did not consider keeping eyelids open a priority, I looked around at Upnor and tried to make an assessment. If Gravesend had been a seaside town beside a miniature ocean, Upnor was a seaside village. According to Maisie, the ocean lapping against a tiny beach at the end of Upnor's one short, narrow street, was called the Medway. While the Thames is like a coster, always ready to trade in anything with anyone, the Medway is more a military river, full of men o' war sailing under shore fort guns. Thames tides bring things in: Medway tides run in the opposite direction, carrying battleships and soldiers out. All the warehouses we passed seemed to contain materials for fighting, not trading. I preferred the Thames.

That was my last thought before collapsing into a chair outside an Upnor inn. Shame to say, Maisie was obliged to fetch the refreshments, given my state of incapacity. We rested for an hour, after which, over the last section to Chatham, my legs turned the crank by habit and little else. The one thing that kept me going was the knowledge that in this unwelcoming place, part town, part barracks, I would have Maisie to myself. Chatham would be my Verona, my Paris.

We cycled to a long terrace of town houses, standing to attention near the navy dock. It looked as though they had stood this way for a long time, the anticipated inspection never coming, uniforms becoming ragged in rain and sun. Here, after locking our bicycles in a lean-to at the end of a tumbledown back yard, Maisie led me to the door of what she said was our theatrical digs.

The door stood dusty and peeling, late afternoon sunlight scrubbing across battered panels like ash soap, bleaching what little colour had not already flaked off. This unpromising door swung open, to reveal Eddie, looking especially Byronic.

"My God, the cruelty,' he said when his eyes laid on me. "Looks like you really did cop a packet from the toshers this time."

"No, once again, it is simply the effects of cycling. What are you doing here? I thought this was me running for my life, not you."

"We came down on the train. I'd recommend it."

"Would you indeed."

"You must have been too preoccupied with getting ready for your cycling trip. But as I said back in London, we want to combine your flight from danger with an out of town concert. We are working on an idea called a tour. It involves taking the band to performances in various places. That way we whip up interest for a kind of photo album of recorded songs which people can buy, and play at home on the music machines we will sell them. This is our first practice run."

"You have it all worked out, don't you, Eddie."

"It's not me as has it worked out, Tim."

Maisie did a little bow. Eddie put an arm around her shoulders and escorted her inside. I hesitated for a moment, hands on hips, looking down at the floor. Was it my imagination or did my hands have to be on my hips, to support them in making my last few steps into the house?

CHAPTER 15

Chatham? Not a nice place. I'm not saying Blue Anchor Yard is perfect, but at least back at the Yard we have people who are not just navy or army. Most of us are traders. We have sailors too of course, being hard by St Katherine's Docks, but those sailors are traders themselves in their way, working merchant ships. In trade, you have to get on with other people, because otherwise they are less inclined to deal with you. I know that sounds simple, but many don't grasp it. Trade in London, even at its toughest, is not dog eat dog. If you want to meet a group of people who care for their fellows, then I would introduce you to the costers of London. Look at me, a young cove provided with his education through Rawbone's pearly charity money. And the pearlies look after a lot of people much more deserving than myself.

Compare this with Chatham, a town full of sailors and soldiers charged with dying for their country, when the town does nothing to put you in the frame of mind for making such a sacrifice. People who live here are lifted out of the normal run of trade, which rewards civility. When they go out to work, they don't have to win their customers over, just despatch them. Rawbone once told me about the famous admiral, Lord Nelson, knowing men as served under him. Nelson, who sits on a massive column in London, was the worst captain you could imagine, always ready with a beating, always ready to take the successes of others as his own. He was no coster. It was illegal to leave his employ. Men had no choice but to endure and hate him.

Maybe it isn't so accidental that next door to Chatham is

a quaint little village called Rochester, just a single street of old England with a massive cathedral built by the same fellow who was responsible for the Tower of London. Rochester has byways, cubbies, coffee houses and an air of gentility, sitting not a few hundred feet from the goings-on of the Lord Nelson pub in Chatham High Street. Rochester plays the part of idealised English life, which is worth defending. Chatham is soldiers, sailors, whores, drink, crime. Who would want to die for that?

Our first concert was to be at a place on the border between these two places of contrast. Eddie showed me the venue with a sense of pride, waving up at a grand building, called The Jolly Companions, a rectangular, brick-built affair with five Georgian windows and the sort of fussily recessed central door that a policeman might find himself obliged to guard. This outwardly respectable structure stood on a street some way up-slope from the river.

"But, Eddie," I pleaded, "why, why, why did you choose Chatham? If the people in this town don't like us they'll just kill us and be done with it."

"We'll be fine. The folk here spend their working days under the lash. When off duty, they will be more accepting of entertainment that breaks the rules. Just wait until they hear Bells of Hell. They'll love it."

Unconvinced, I continued to remonstrate as we walked along the sunken road that is Chatham High Street. High Street could hardly be described as a fitting name, for what was a low, skulking place, dug in beneath a hill inclining to the Medway. It lacked the trading bustle of London. Shop fronts sat back in shadow, sad looking women shuffling between them, as though hiding from possible snipers in an enormous trench. Only the inns were busy. The Admiral Rodney's bay windows appeared to bulge outwards from a drunken press inside. At intervals the pressure became too much, at which point some soused troublemakers would burst through the door with a publican's frothy-mouthed dog held on a rope behind them.

"You say," I continued, "that these people like to break rules in their leisure time. But the fact is, they only do that in certain accepted ways. Their misbehaviour is so predictable - all that drinking, consorting and fighting night after night. You would think it would get boring, but they can't get enough of it. And you know why? Because these people are not of an adventurous and curious frame of mind. Anything really out of the ordinary, anything that is different to tried and tested British misbehaviour, they will throw bottles at."

"You worry too much, Timmy. In the entertainment business we face this every night. You write the lyrics and leave the rest to us."

CHAPTER 16

The first night at the Jolly Companions, my worries of audience attack did indeed turn out to be groundless. But that was because there were only three sailors in the audience.

We had two small steam engines on wheels in the back yard at full steam, maintained by Smalt. He'd connected up our instruments to cables, running them through to the stage. You could almost hear the electricity humming in that big, open, almost empty hall.

"Don't worry," said Eddie looking out at the sad prospect of three lost sailors. "This is a try-out, so let's just get on with it."

Striding on stage, Eddie raised a hand in salutation.

"Hello Chatham! We have got something new for you tonight. So glad you could make it."

The sailors were at this point conducting a kind of three-legged race with four legs, arms around shoulders, careering across the space of the hall, just because they had it all to themselves. I have seen something similar with young lads cavorting in an open space at Borough Market during the moving of some stalls.

"This is a song we call Bells of Hell."

At this point the first 'musician' to play was in fact none other than Smalt, who manipulated his off-stage machinery to produce the recorded sound of Big Ben, booming out from noise boxes. The sound made a St James's Park of the Jolly Companions. Our three tars staggered to a halt, and like ships manoeuvring to form a line of battle, they swung to face us.

Their faces revealed men who had become aware of gunfire at sea. As Belle's lazy riff played across Big Ben's beat, my skin prickled, just as it had on that dark night in London. Those incredible opening chords made me think of a clever drawing I once saw in Almanac's parlour, of a steam ship with the side taken off, so you could see all the decks stacked on top of one another, the whole machine moving at full power through a transparent ocean.

This pictorial thought seemed apposite for our three sailors, who appeared to be watching a sight no less shocking than a ship sailing on the sea whilst open to the waves across one entire side. And when the final chords of Bells of Hell faded away, they began cheering in a way which I assumed they must have learned when their ship had triumphed over some enemy vessel, and they now realised that rather than sinking in a flaming wreck, they would live to see another day. Their reception of every other song in a five song set was the same.

When we reached the end, our sailors didn't quite know how to comport themselves. Because there were so few of them, there wasn't the usual gap between audience and performers.

"What did you think?" asked Eddie in a conversational tone as he began dismantling his microphone stand.

The sailors looked at each other, trying I think to establish rank in this unforeseen situation. Who was to be their captain? Cometh the hour, cometh the man. Our fellow on the left stepped forward.

"We thought we were whistling up a wind with you lots, but...." The man struggled with his vocabulary. "But that was.... good."

"Thanks," said Eddie.

Our first audience looked at each other, unable, it appeared, to think of anything else to say. Maybe they felt intimidated because the band outnumbered the audience. That's the military mind for you. They swayed into the wider world of Chatham.

The second night was different. By some kind of military semaphore, word had got around. The Jolly Companions was rammed tight as a troop ship. I was sheltering in the stage wings, an observer of proceedings, looking out at a turbulent sea of faces. There were a lot of women in the audience, so many in fact that I assumed the entire working-girl population of Chatham was here. For what must have been their own personal safety in such a crowd, they formed a phalanx to our left, from where they called out comments to Eddie about his good looks and his Byron fashion choices. At this point it was hard to tell if those comments were barbed or admiring. The girls were kind of hedging bets at the moment, waiting to see how things would go.

Eddie stood before a microphone atop a pole, similar to those back at the studio, speaking in a way that he had been working on, which seemed to combine street and palace, and thus might include everyone.

"Good evening Chatham, how you all doing tonight?"

Chatham it seemed was doing quite well, whilst remaining suspicious and guarded about what it had come to see. The population wouldn't storm the stage and beat us up yet, but reserved the right to do so.

As on the previous evening, we opened with Bells of Hell. Our recreated Big Ben rang out its midnight apocalypse, Maisie playing across the beats, Whistle adding his repeated, downward moving three notes, and then - almost stopping my heart - Long Tom's drums joining in.

I heard someone shout:

"Holy mother of Mary."

There are only mute words at my disposal for the purposes of description. It was like plugging all the ancient music of humanity, from way back in Africa, straight into the output of all the factories in northern England. As for our audience, the sound of those midnight bells appeared to be ringing to warn of imminent invasion of these shores. The military went onto a violent war footing, happy that the enemy was at hand at last, and joyful that somehow they could have this feeling without experiencing the fear of approaching death. They seemed to be victorious in a battle where there didn't have to be any losers.

Eddie followed Bells of Hell with our songs about fashion, unhappy monarchs, music hall women, and scary monsters. By now, electricity was flowing through our instruments, through us, and our juiced-up audience. Finally, we came to something new, which I had written a few days before, trying to expand our song list.

Memories of composing that new piece stole me away from the concert chaos for a few moments. We had been sitting around in candle light in our Chatham digs, which were not what you would describe as luxurious. Prince Edward had only released a bare minimum of funds to cover the trip, worried as he was about searching questions from watchful authorities. I was used to accommodation that fell short of palatial. What I wasn't used to was the feeling of careless neglect that came from the fact that men only ever bivouacked in houses like this. There were not enough women to make Chatham into a civilised place to live.

Eddie, of course was ignoring the poverty, looking as resplendent as ever in velvet, fopping around with Maisie on a decrepit chaise longue.

"You are a real doodie, Eddie," crooned Maisie.

This was a serious, formidable young woman, who had spent a life of discipline under hard, uncaring tutors. And now with her krooman band, she could lean towards the frothy and giggly. And she aimed to do so.

"What a doodie you are," she reiterated, delighted to be carefree and adventurous. And if you are reading this in Scotland or the colonies, or the future, a doodie is what we in London call a dandy, like Eddie.

"Doodie, doodie doo... Can you make a song out of that, Tim?" asked Whistle, strumming out a pattern on his non-electric guitar.

I think his question was the ironic sort of challenge which assumes the answer has to be no.

"Of course he can," defended Belle, perched next to Whistle, her fingers jumping from one fret pattern to another.

I liked the word doodie, but didn't like the "e" sound on the end. It made the word sound juvenile. We were staging a musical revolution, and a baby-sounding word just wasn't right for people doing that. It also didn't sound right in the mouth of a woman like Maisie. So, I just took the word and changed it a little.

"Dudes. That's us. Here we all are then. We're the dudes."

"That's a song," cried Eddie. "Get to work."

Now, only a few days later, we were on this stage with Eddie yelling at the audience:

"Hey dude. I want to hear your story, I want to know who you are."

He was picking out individual members of the crowd.

"Hey, I see ye, you with one arm, you with a tattoo across your face. I see ye. Come on. I want to see what you're doing."

Rehearsals and our concert to three people the day before had not prepared me for what now happened. Everyone in the crowd reached out to whoever was next to them and put their arms around that stranger's shoulders. They were mostly hardened killers or whores, and yet as a body here they were, swaying along with our song. Some of them were crying! The girls even put their arms around some of the men, as though they were friends, or brothers. How likely was that to happen? I wouldn't have believed it if I didn't see it with my own eyes. We had made them feel like dudes, special individuals, who enjoyed unique fellowship. What a feeling.

As an encore we played the fashion song, which brought us to the point that Eddie assumed was the attentional capacity of our audience. They'd probably want to be off to the Lord Nelson now, or some flop house. There was no real bowing, which I thought was traditional following a musical entertainment. Instead, Eddie's salute involved much waving and holding of his arms above his head. I noticed his hand do a salute where index and little finger stuck upwards, while middle fingers were held down by the thumb. I think he had seen Italians doing this on the docks as a sign of good luck.

"Thank you, Chatham. You have been legendary. Goodnight."

Then an awful turmoil erupted. It was a mixture of booing, jeering, cheering and screaming.

Eddie retreated, looking pale under his makeup. We went into conference.

"I thought they liked us," said Eddie.

"Typical," moaned Whistle. "We finally start playing some amazing music and all we get are ignorant sailors and their tarts. Pearls before swine."

"They ain't so bad," remarked Long Tom, still relaxed behind his drums, reluctant to leave.

Belle and Maisie marched into the debate, Belle holding the neck of her idle guitar up beside her smooth, lemon hair, Maisie's instrument slung low, so that the neck hung pointing towards the stage.

"What's going on?" asked Maisie. "I can't tell. Are they happy or sad?"

"They're happy," said Belle, taking a cup-half-full approach to life. "I just don't think they want us to stop. They love us."

"I think she's right," shouted Long Tom. Only Tom had the ability to shout in a calm manner, like he was talking in a noisy pub.

The manager of the Jolly Companions was down the front trying to stop a stage invasion, his voice staccato against a wailing, screaming, background.

"That's it. No. No. No. That's it now, lads. I mean it."

"We have to play some more," I yelled at Eddie. "Play the dude song again. Keep them as happy as you can, while I try to find a way to get us out."

Eddie hesitated, looked down at his velvet and lace outfit, from which he seemed to gain strength. He marched stage front, as though this had been his plan all along.

"Alright Chatham. We've had a very heavy request to do another one for you, for you.... dudes."

There was a kind of eruption. I can only think of it as a few thousand writers all finding out at the same time that Chapman and Hall was to publish their work.

Slipping backstage, I made my way to the stage door, the crowd noise now a party in a distant room, somehow making me feel very alone. Out in one of Chatham's typical dark, sunken, trench-like streets, I shouted:

"Cab."

A couple of inebriated sailors staggering by, pointed at me in a manner which suggested there were two or three of me to point at.

"Maybe 'e sinks he's in London town."

The sailors stumbled onwards, lost in their false world where they had to kill people rather than win them over to what you had to offer. They wobbled straight into a small group of girls bursting out of the door of the Jolly Companions. This group, intent at getting a jump on their fellows in offering violent, post-show congratulations, was a harbinger of things to come.

I realised there were no cabs in this place, no such civilised conveniences that a lady or gentleman might call upon to ease their journey. How were we going to get out of this? Gone now was any idea that we would just be able to walk from the Jolly Companions and make a perambulation to the Bull Inn, Rochester, where an after-show gay-and-hearty waited for us. We would have to use the cart that Smalt had arranged for equipment.

I slipped inside, making a wending return to backstage, crowd noise bursting down the narrow corridors like a flood through a storm drain. Standing in the stage wings, I made desperate gestures to Belle to come and take my report. She sidled over to me, playing those stacked, steam-ship-deck chords all the while.

"It's no good, there are no cabs in this godforsaken town. And there's no way we can risk leaving on foot."

"Of course there are no cabs. This isn't London."

"Our best chance is if Smalt gets us out on the equipment wagon. Be ready to move when I say."

I ran up to Smalt, who bent over his turbines, appeared oblivious to the chaos around him.

"Smalt. We need to get the band out on your cart."

"But where will the machinery go, Mr Tim? The master made it clear it was not to be harmed."

"But we can't have the musicians harmed."

"The master gave no direction about that."

Smalt's eyes went back to the turbine, trying to find comfort in its regular operation. I continued my efforts of persuasion.

"What good is machinery if there are no people able to use it? We will come back for it."

Smalt engaged in an inward struggle, as the Earth's crust must undergo in those exotic parts of the world where earthquakes are building up but haven't quite happened yet.

"There must be a lock-up where we can put the gear, until it is safe to get back here and pick it up. I will stay behind and help you with that."

"You go with the others. You is a sensitive writer. You will not cope with danger."

"I'm not sensitive. Why do people keep saying that? Writers are tough."

Smalt looked at me with pity in his eyes.

"You get everyone out the back of the theatre and I will look after the rest."

"Good. I'll be back."

I grabbed a white-faced stagehand.

"Where's the manager of this place?"

"He's not 'ere."

"What do you mean? I need to talk to him."

"He's gorn mate. I should do the same, but I want to hear that dude song again. I never seen nothing like this act. Are all your theatricals in London like this?"

"Listen, you've got to help get us out safely."

"What can I do? I ain't in charge of nothing."

"That doesn't matter. You stayed, because you know this is special, not like that coward of a manager. You have to help us, so we will live for another show. You want another show, don't you?"

"I surely do. Is there maybe a ticket in it?"

"Yes, two tickets for you and a friend, but please help us. We're going to get out on a cart we used for our gear. Is there somewhere we can stow the gear until we can come back for it?"

"I'll open up the store."

The band had sung the dudes song three times, when my stagehand tapped me on the shoulder. Eddie began an a cappella, as a rear guard action. By now, the audience had taken over the singing for themselves, so it was not so obvious that the band was melting away backstage, skulking along those tight corridors, out through a door to the yard behind the theatre, where Smalt held nervous horses by their bridles. Even with our deception, the yard was now filling with hysterical Chatham folk all intent on getting a closer look at this phenomenon they had just witnessed.

Eddie, last out, was yelling at me:

"Where will the equipment go? Maisie says she won't leave it behind."

"Get in the cart," I yelled. "I will help Smalt look after the gear. Get in now."

At this point, I felt a familiar sense that arms that usually whacked hammers on anvils had grabbed me. Rather than throwing me into the Thames, these arms threw me into the cart where I landed in an ungainly fashion. Maisie came flying in after me. Eddie, Belle, Whistle and Long Tom all climbed in under their own power.

The horses now made the decision that enough was enough. I assume these nags, hired locally, were trained to look war in the face and keep trotting on regardless. Even so, this musical affray was too much for them. They dashed off down the street, their handler only giving an illusion of control, because his horses happened to want the same thing he did.

After a terrifying journey, during which swinging sideways was often indistinguishable from moving forward, we ended up at Rochester's Bull Inn, the cart clattering through the carriage entrance, while some of Prince Edward's men hauled double-doors closed behind us.

Maisie paced about the bar, announcing that she was going back to the Jolly Companions to recover her precious devices. Eddie pleaded with her not to go, taking an hour before he came round to agreeing it might be safe to return to the scene of our ambivalent triumph.

We climbed aboard the same cart on which we had made our escape, and attempted a cautious return. It was Long Tom who had to take the reins this time, the military equestrian fellow who had driven us out, no longer volunteering for active service. The horses were also skittish, and required much of Tom's calm tongue clicking and patting of necks to consent to their mission. In the event, we found the Jolly Companions abandoned, its audience washed off to other amusements. With trepidation, Maisie took the lead in pushing open the stage door. And then, thanks to all the fates, we found Smalt outside the lock up, a man who had never left his post. Maisie marched up to Smalt's wilting frame, and gave him one of those hugs with which he was so uncomfortable.

"I has never experienced anything like this before," said Smalt in a strangled voice. "I would have died rather than let anything happen to Miss Maisie's inventions."

After assisting Smalt in retrieving noise boxes, instruments with associated accoutrements, we all drove together back to our digs. Here I sat in a shocked daze while the others seemed unwilling to accept a sudden move from chaos to peace. Anything I write will sound awkward, because we went from one state of things straight into another. There was no polite foreshadowing of scenes, no easing the reader between one setting and another. We went from an intense state of joy, mayhem and anxiety, to sitting in a dilapidated lodging house in Chatham. If this was a switch of scenes in a book, I wouldn't have accepted it. Whistle for one was not accepting it. He and Eddie seemed determined to make my narrative more realistic by transferring a small part of the concert to our digs, managing the transfer in their riotous behaviour. There was drinking, carousing and carrying on. Long Tom bore witness in his quiet manner, not the main centre of trouble, but not willing to wholly accept the abrupt shock of going quietly into that morning after. Maisie and Belle climbed down from their emotional intensity by stages. I didn't get to bed until about 3am, when fatigue finally defeated the extremity of what we had just been through. Was this my life now?

CHAPTER 17

In the same way that our Chatham concert sat awkwardly with its evening after, I now felt a profound disassociation of events. I lay looking at a smooth, white ceiling wondering what had happened. The reason for lying here was not clear, and nothing seemed to have led up to it. I opened my eyes and there it was, a ceiling strangely far away.

"How are you, Tim?"

"Belle?"

"Yes, luvvie. It's your Belle."

"Belle....?"

Disjointed bell themed thoughts went through my mind. Bells of Hell... Alexander Graham Bell... Big Ben booming out in the night. What were all these bells? They all seemed to be ringing at once.

"You've had a bump on the head, darlin'."

"I have? Belle. I remember you."

"That's good."

There was a silence. And what was the first question you might expect me to ask? Where was I? How did I get here? What happened? Not a bit of it.

"Tell me, Belle, are you going to marry Whistle?"

The hand, which I now realised was dabbing a cold cloth against my head, hesitated in its ministrations.

"I am not going to marry Whistle."

"Why not?"

"Because he is a stupid man."

"So, why do you stay with him?"

"I work with him. He is a very good kroo guitarist. There aren't many of those around."

"I see. Belle?"

"Yes, dear?"

"Will you marry me then?"

"You have your eye on Maisie, unfortunately for you."

"I do? Who's she?"

"You don't remember?"

"I don't. I'm working forward. I have reached you and Whistle and Long Tom, and rehearsing at the Wilton."

"How are things going for us then?"

"Not very well. Nobody likes our songs."

"Well keep going just a bit longer and things get better."

I lay and looked at that ceiling, which once again seemed much further away than a ceiling should be - also smoother and cleaner.

"Am I in a palace?"

"No, dear. You're in a house in Birdcage Walk."

"Birdcage Walk? But I live in Blue Anchor Yard."

"Not any longer."

"Oh, now I recall a ring. And two royals called Victoria?"

"I'm afraid so."

Maisie then entered my recollections. It began with a sound, a kind of many-layered musical eruption. Then to go with this sound, there came an image of a jacket the colour of cucumber ice cream.

"Maisie. I remember. The genius girl?"

"That's right. She's busy, rehearsing."

"Oh... Shouldn't you be rehearsing? I remember you telling me sometime that you preferred music to men."

"Yes, I did say that. But that doesn't mean I can't take care of you, Tim."

In the sort of way that fancy French artists paint impressions rather than solid things, there were memories of our concert.

"I remember Chatham, Belle. Are we famous now?"

"No. We got back to London, and it's as if nothing happened. Maybe steam-powered music is just not possible in people's minds yet. There was nothing in the papers, not even in the stage press."

"I think I'm remembering more now."

"That's good. I thought you were proper hurt."

I managed to raise my head, which proved to be very sore, and look around.

"Are none of the others concerned?"

"No, Tim. I won't do no sugar coating for you."

"After all those lyrics I wrote."

"They're just waiting for you to get up and write some more."

"Well thanks for staying with me, Belle."

This remark was greeted with continued tender dabbing of cool flannel upon forehead.

I remembered coming back to Birdcage Walk from Chatham, sneaking through Victoria Station using elaborate placings of baggage carts and other members of our party, one of whom seemed to be Prince Edward in disguise.

Prince Edward? What was the heir to the throne doing in my recollections?

"I remember the Prince of Wales for some reason. I don't think you should stop bathing my forehead just yet."

Belle refreshed the flannel's chill.

"No, you're alright. The Prince of Wales is our sponsor."

"That's not my imagination?"

Belle just kept on dabbing, which I took as agreement that my recollections were accurate.

"Belle, I think it was just my fancy that I had a chance with Maisie. She prefers Eddie. It's taken a bang on the head to bring that home to me."

"Now, while we're on the topic of Maisie and Eddie there is something I want to tell you quietly, which I think you need to know."

"Really?"

"Maisie might be Prince Edward's daughter."

"Oh yes. I remember Whistle saying he thought that."

"Well, Prince Edward may also be Eddie's father."

"What?"

"Prince Edward has women all over the place. He was involved with Maisie's mother, while they were in India. And there is also talk of a high born Indian woman. We can't be sure, but how do you think Eddie and Maisie met? How did Prince Edward, of all people, hear about their strange musical project? And why is he so interested in helping them?"

"Yes, I hadn't really thought about that."

"My advice is to stay well out."

"Yes, I think you're right, Belle."

All this advice was accompanied by the application of that cooling flannel. Once I had settled my thoughts down after Belle's suppositions, I came back to the question that really should have come first.

"So, what happened to me?"

"They wanted another out of town concert, just to make sure we were on the right lines, without attracting too much attention. To check a possible venue, you and Maisie went out to Beckenham. You rode your bicycle. I am here to tell you not to ride that contraption anymore."

"Did I fall off again?"

"You did."

"Why do I do it?"

"To impress Maisie."

"Belle. I think I've had some sense knocked into me."

"No more riding just to impress Maisie. You went to a new recreation ground in Croydon Road. Maisie thought it would suit."

"Well this is nice," said Maisie in misty memory, swinging off her bike and gliding along, balanced by one foot upon a pedal. Trying the same trick, I fell onto forgiving grass, formed into an attractive oval area by symmetrical paths. This clearly wasn't the fatal fall that put me in bed. I remembered sitting up on soft turf, as Maisie came to a halt a little way ahead. She didn't hurry back towards me. From my sitting position, I looked around at a place that she judged as perfect. It was a suburban park, where nannies strode along curving paths with other people's babies in perambulators. I didn't know if this place quite met the mark. Still, with music as new as ours, where did meet the mark? Was a place like Chatham the most suitable? Who knows? At least Beckenham was more respectable. Looking again, I decided that this grass oval could define a performance area, with our stage at the far end.

"This will do," said the Maisie of cloudy recollection.

She had by this time ambled back towards me, and I'd regained my feet. It was a lovely day of early summer.

"Let's get back to Birdcage Walk to tell Eddie," said Maisie, doing her one foot on the pedal thing again, pushing with the other to get speed.

Recent evidence might have suggested that while I was much better on a bicycle, any attempt to mimic such advanced manoeuvres would be foolish. But love is something that makes us do things that bring us closer to our beloved, even when doing so makes us look ridiculous in the eyes of said beloved. I tried the one foot thing. It was at the moment of attempted transfer of weight across a moving bike to get both feet on the pedals that it happened. At least I assume it did, because this was my last memory of Beckenham, before the scene changed.

I was floating, high up above the Earth, listening to a voice calling me.

"This is Blue Anchor Yard calling Tosher Tim. This is Blue Anchor Yard calling Tosher Tim. Eat your gellied eels and put your flat cap on."

I realised how far from home I had come. Maybe it wasn't all that far in miles, but events had still taken me to the dark side of the moon. In my short lifetime, London had changed, so that the boy I once was would have trouble finding his way around in some parts of the city. Even if someone continued to live in their place of birth, staying in the same house, in the same street, with no thought of moving away, there was no protection against change breaking in and stealing you away. We played the music of a world galloping onwards faster than Flying Fox at Newmarket, the music of young people. But even for youngsters, time must fly onwards, leaving them older. They in their turn would be taking nostalgic refuge in the once modish music they grew up with.

I was lost, generally speaking, and also specifically in seeming to find myself floating above the Earth. No doubt you, my clever reader, has realised my sense of aerial navigation had nothing to do with a fanciful Maisie-designed airship, and everything to do with a bang on the head. At the time, this actual concussion was a small detail, a symptom rather than a cause. My daze was simply an extension of the general oddity of life before my head impacted asphalt.

The morning following my first day under Belle's care, I awoke against pillows that betrayed care of arrangement. Those pillows made me confident of continuing attention. I called for maybe a little breakfast. It was a surprise when Long Tom poked his head around the door.

"Hello, Tom. Where's Belle?"

"Maisie wanted Belle and the others to look at the venue in Beckenham. They've just left."

"They have?"

"Maisie said you were fine, but Belle was insistent I stay and keep an eye."

I had no idea whether Long Tom would be a reliable source of breakfast. He seemed interested in food, but only in eating, not preparing. In the event I did receive a bowl of runny porridge.

After serving breakfast, Long Tom disappeared, the restful silence only broken by the distant sound of metronomically precise, yet indefinable rhythms.

I tried to console myself with the thought that at least a writer like myself always has their writing, even when struck down by bicycling disaster. That was all well and good until I found that my pen had nowhere to go on an empty page in a notebook, resting on the coverlet of my sick bed. In Blue Anchor Yard, it had always been a trial to find ink or paper. At least my new life gave me copious quantities of both. How ironic that all of those expensive sheets now only served to mock my lack of inspiration. They seemed to be making petulant demands for a novel, when I couldn't even remember that song about Tosher Tim sending a telegram home to Blue Anchor Yard.

Trying to get back into that floaty frame of mind, I recalled those soldiers at Chatham. I wondered if they were dreaming of places faraway, or wishing they could go home, or whether those two feelings were muddled up in that odd place where they lived, which was neither England nor a foreign land. I think the future might be a place where people will feel more and more like those soldiers. What if people went to live on other worlds in airships? Those other worlds would be their home. Would they look at our world and think of it as a different star? Maybe everywhere is home in the end.

I decided to change Tosher Tim into Captain Tim.

Bear with me, patient reader. This is what happens when you lie in bed after banging your head.

Now we were recording our music, the audience for it could be anywhere, near or far in space and time. For my song it seemed fitting that Captain Tim spends one verse calling home, while in the next, someone at home calls to him. The effect for a person listening is to give the feeling that they are both faraway and home at the same time. I called my collection of lines, Captain Tim's Odd Odyssey.

I showed the lyrics to Eddie when he got back. He snatched the page and began to read.

"Can I have some warming soup?" I asked.

Without taking his eyes off the sheet of paper, Eddie walked out of my room.

"Tim wants some soup," he called to no one in particular, still not stopping in his reading.

CHAPTER 18

Belle, back from her trip continued to attend me, which was a relief. After jesting about seeing a dent in one of the Beckenham park pavements, about the size and shape of my head, she passed on positive news of how rehearsal was going down in our basement studio. Sometimes from my bed, I would hear faint sounds of music. It was a comfort.

One evening a few days later, I awoke and sensed that things were different. I felt better for one thing. But it wasn't just that. There had been a shift in the house, an ominous change. After all this time resting, my legs seemed to have assumed that their services were no longer required. Now it was necessary to force their reluctant resumption of duty. Standing beside the bed, I looked down and saw floorboards. It appeared that someone had stolen the carpet. That was taking advantage. What a dastardly thing to do. And also, what an odd way to be dastardly. Who would take someone's floor rug? Taking a look around it was clear that everything else you would expect to see in a songwriter's bedroom was still here - my desk with ink, nibs and piles of paper covered with lyrics I'd been working on. So the thief just wanted the rug then? It didn't make sense and made me wonder if I was yet quite better.

I thought Belle said everyone was rehearsing in the basement, but all was quiet.

"Belle..."

No answer.

Would I ever see Belle again? Maybe the carpet thieves had

carried her away.

There was a pitcher of water on my bedside table. I poured myself a glass and drank it off.

"Anybody here?"

There was no answer to my call.

It was no good staying here, quaking on bare boards. There was very little water left in the pitcher. And soon I would be needing food.

Had Maisie gone too far with her inventions causing something outlandish to happen? Maybe she made all those denials about time machines just to cover up the fact that she had, in fact, made a time machine, which had transported me and the house back to some ancient era. Almanac had once leant me a book by Edward Drinker Cope describing prehistoric lizard creatures. If I looked out of the window, would there be a terrifying vision of a giant reptile eating my carpet? I pulled back the curtain to be comforted by the usual trees separating our house from Birdcage Walk. St James's Park spread out in all its glorious familiarity beyond those leaf canopies. Everything seemed as it had been before - except for the carpet. Oh, for my old life where people stole normal things like money or jewellery.

There was no creak when I pulled the door open. And if you were expecting one I'd just like to say that this story has no aspirations to the gothic, with clichés to indicate to my more nervously disposed reader that this account is just a story. The hallway carpet was missing. See what I mean? That was scarier than a creaking door. With a creaking door, you know where you are.

Bare wooden stairs led down to the ground floor.

"Hello. Anyone?"

After five anxious minutes, my survey of the ground floor was complete. There was no one here. Every room had its carpets and rugs stripped. There was only one more part of the house as yet un-investigated, and that was the basement studio. Exploring there required walking down a dark stairwell.

I began the descent, coming to a halt on the last step. I could hear very faint sounds of music, as though coming from underground. Had the studio collapsed, with Maisie's equipment continuing to play music in the wreckage? What really prevented me from running away at this moment was the worry that maybe Belle was injured and requiring help. She had brought me soup and mopped my brow during illness. The least I could do was make sure she hadn't become the victim of some kind of futuristic catastrophe.

"For Belle," were my words of bravery as I pushed open the studio door.

And as the door swung open, music washed over me. There they all were, about half way through my song, Captain Tim's Odd Odyssey. There also was my bedroom rug, cut up and laid out in wooden frames upon the far wall. Similar frames containing all the other house carpets covered wall and ceiling, and even the inner face of the door I'd just opened.

A few minutes later, I sat beside Smalt in the control room.

"The carpet soaks up sound, Mr Tim. The microphones were picking up echoes bouncing back from plaster walls and making for a muddy effect. There was also leakage getting in from outside. Mr Blackwell directed me to take all the carpets and put them on the walls down here. It's a crude measure, which we will improve upon in time. You never woke when we took the carpet out of your room. Anyways, it has worked to a fair degree."

"Well, it gave me the shy bladder I can tell you."

"What did?"

"The carpet disappearing."

"You're a sensitive one. But that's alright because you're a man of letters."

I thought about arguing, but the necessary strength wasn't there. Let him believe I was sensitive. It seemed to be what people wanted.

Smalt manipulated his controls. Whilst doing so, he spoke into a mouthpiece, the sort of thing you would find aboard an ironclad to carry commands from bridge to engine room.

"Alright, let's go for a take."

"A take? What's one of those?"

"Oh that's just me, Mr Tim. Pay it no mind."

"No, tell me, what is a take?"

Moving levers, Smalt clearly didn't really have time for an answer, but he shot one off out of charity.

"Well you see, I 'spose I just started calling each individual recording a take, because I'm taking the sound and putting it on the tape."

A further lever clunked into place.

"And why is Long Tom sitting in that strange box with windows?"

"That's what we call an isolation booth. Miss Maisie says it was invented by Thomas Watson, an assistant of Alexander Graham Bell's, during demonstrations of the telephone. It allows me to isolate the loud sound of Tom's drums so I can balance it against the other instruments and vocals."

"And what are those odd things on Belle's head?"

I was referring to a pair of earpieces, which looked like they were from an Alexander Graham Bell telephone, set within a flexible truss-like affair, which had adjusted itself to sit snug against Belle's shapely ears.

"That is something we are calling headphones. They are based on the Edison speaker, which Graham Bell and Edison are developing at the United Telephone Company. I imagine they would not be pleased if they knew. Anyways, we use them to play the accompaniment to Belle, so that her singing can be isolated and then mixed to give the purest result."

"What will it all sound like when it's put together? Will we hear the gaps?"

"Don't you worry 'bout no gaps, Mr Tim."

Whistle played the opening chords of Captain Tim's Odd Odyssey. Eddie was singing, with some great accompaniment from both Whistle and Belle on guitar.

"Just Miss Belle now," called Smalt through the speaker tube. Eddie sat to one side on a tall stool looking foppish, while Belle sang her section.

"Very impressive, Smalt. Tell me, why do you talk to them through a tube?"

"So that no noise I make in here is picked up upon the recording."

Feeling unwell again, I returned to my bed. My final emergence took place a few days later, by which time Belle was telling me to stop malingering. It was time to get better, so I did my best to oblige.

And then down in the studio I finally listened to the result of everyone's work, all those tries and takes, which had been going on while I lay abed. Smalt was right. It all came together in one song, which had the most incredible clarity and beauty of sound. This was the best we could be. I know it was us, and yet somehow it wasn't, because we could never attain to that perfection. I was the writer and the audience as well, like Captain Tim listening to a message, whilst also sending it out.

CHAPTER 19

The trip to Beckenham, for our next concert, was upon us. I was obliged to pull a flat cap down over my eyes and board a train. This was now considered a lesser risk than putting me on a bicycle. A theatrical moustache supplied by Eddie, helped in the scramble through Victoria, though the giggling this disguise provoked in some of my fellows, was a risk to security. Once on the train I unpeeled my wretched, fake facial hair, whilst shuffling along the corridor trying to find a compartment. It was Eddie who gestured towards one particular sliding door, as though he had been negotiating for a table at a good restaurant and had been given the nod. There was a rush to grab the compartment, no doubt resulting from some atavistic desire to stake out boundaries in a new and unfamiliar environment. In the confusion, I found myself in an all-fellows compartment. The girls were next door.

Smalt came in last, carrying what looked like a small suitcase rendered in wood, with a lattice-work grill dominating one side.

"Can't that go with the rest of the luggage?" moaned Whistle, who was obliged to tuck his legs in, to allow Smalt and his odd load to proceed to a free seat by the window.

"Do you not desire the window seat?" enquired Smalt.

"My eyes have not been designed to see objects passing before me at unnatural speeds. It provokes a severe nausea and flux in my system."

"As you wish, sir."

Smalt sat down, placing the device in his charge upon the floor.

"It's acting up, Mr Whistle. The store for electrical charge is causing difficulties."

Smalt began to fiddle with diminutive levers on a panel, left of the grill. Whistle studied this activity with suspicion.

"What is that thing anyway?"

"It is a device we are trying, for the play-back of music from magnetised tape rather than record discs. It might serve as something that can more easily be taken from place to place."

The train shuddered under us, before settling into a calmer rhythm as we pulled out of Victoria. And then just when it seemed reasonable to relax in our new personal train compartment, the door slid open and instincts rebelled against that worst of all contingencies when staking out new territory - an interloper. For a moment, I had visions of one of Old Ma's heavies come to get me. But the dark suit, aggressive umbrella, and belligerent bowler, suggested a different kind of heavy, the sort who maybe works in Whitehall.

The dour disapproval of the man passed over my head, coming to rest on Eddie, who in his usual ankle resting upon opposite knee pose, sat in the manner most conducive to show off his velvet round-me-houses and lacy trappings.

There was only one seat left in the compartment. Whilst any reasonable person would have passed on down the train looking for a quieter spot, this man was not about to give ground to a bunch of young dandies. He set himself in the one remaining seat, opposite me, between Whistle and Long Tom. A look of disdain went one way towards Whistle, followed by a glance of aversion the other way towards Tom, who was doing nothing more threatening than eating some pastries he had picked up at Victoria. There were some crumbs I grant you, but Tom meant no harm to anyone.

A copy of The Times of London, more a blanket than a newspaper, spread itself out between the gent's hands, almost blotting Whistle and Long Tom from view. The insulating properties of this newspaper blanket did not appear to be sufficient, however, because the gentleman soon let out an exasperated sigh, stood up and leant across Whistle to pull closed the open window.

"If I may be so bold…." objected Eddie, who with the benefit of velvet's thermal properties was clearly not feeling any chill just at that moment. "We'd like that left open."

"Well I'd like it closed."

"But there are more of us than you," objected Whistle, "and we would like it open."

"I travel on this train every week, regular as clockwork. As a seasoned, regular traveller I have rights."

"We do too, my good man," objected Eddie. "Ever hear of universal suffrage? One day even women will get the vote."

"Balderdash."

Just at this moment, Smalt's fidgeting with the sound box resulted in an eruption of the opening chords of Bells of Hell.

"Just what is going on here?"

This exclamation of outraged properness accompanied Smalt's effort to quieten down the rebellious sound box.

Before our tormentor could demand any more information, the door slid open to reveal Belle, who despite her youth and good looks, also had the bearing of a headmistress.

"Smalt, please come with me. And please bring your luggage."

"I'll come too," I said, knowing it had been a mistake to go in the compartment with all the boys. No one fancied sitting with the grumpy gent any longer, which meant there was a giggling-and-pushing-squeezing of everybody into the neighbouring compartment. It was like a party. I tried to manoeuvre things so as to be squashed in a corner with Belle, but as the tides of rough and tumble would have it, I ended up sitting on Eddie's velveteen lap.

"So," said Eddie, "I've been meaning to ask you something, Tim, and this seems like a good opportunity. We need a better word for what we do than 'concert'."

"Do we?" I addressed this question to my knees, as twisting around to face Eddie required contortions to which I felt unequal.

"It's not a good word," agreed Belle from the opposite bench.

"What other word is there?"

"I don't know," mused Belle, "something that doesn't make you think of that cove in the bowler hat next door, or fifty people in evening dress playing violins, trumpets and French horns."

"What about engagement?" I ventured.

"Engagement?" mocked Eddie. "Come on, Tim. You're a man of words. You can do better than that."

"Engage... gauge.. What about a gauge?"

"A gauge? That's a thing for measuring steam pressure, isn't it?" This was Long Tom talking through his last pastry.

"True. Gauge...gaig... geg... What about geg?"

"Gig?" said Maisie, seeking clarity.

"No, geg," I enunciated carefully in her direction.

"I thought you said gig. I liked that better."

"Gig...?"

"Gig... It sounds like a kind of dance, or maybe a carriage about to take you for an exciting ride. What about gig, everyone?"

There was a general hum that either suggested agreement,

or at least lack of hostility to the idea.

"We also need a name for our group," piped up Belle. "We need an identity so that people can talk about us and pass us around like a packet of comfits."

"A name for the group? That's an odd idea," said Whistle, who of a sudden had become a musical purist. "Can't we just be us?"

"No, we need a name, to identify our recordings; a brand name, like Pears Soap."

This started a long general conversation with everyone chipping in ideas.

The Steam Engines came from Whistle, The Pistons was Long Tom's idea. I suggested Airship. Belle wanted Lightning. Maisie floated Smoke Stack.

"What about Loud?" said Long Tom.

There was some nodding, mainly from Whistle, who liked the loudness aspect.

"We're not just loud," objected Belle.

"Maybe we are a bunch of creatures who sing," I opined, not knowing where I was going with this line of reasoning. "Maybe we could be called The Starlings, or The Sandpipers, or just The Birds."

"But we make music that is powered by electricity," objected Belle. "The name has to say what we are."

"The Electric Birds?" I ventured.

"Hmmmm."

"Alright, what about creatures who make music with a beat... What about Beatles, spelt b,e,a,t?"

"We can't call ourselves Beatles," declared Belle shuddering. "That's erratic and no mistake."

There was a brittle silence as everyone busted up their brains for a name.

"Let me try something different," said Eddie. "Smalt, what was your mother's favourite colour?"

"Pink, I suppose."

"Tom, what was your mother's maiden name?"

"Floyd."

"Are we going to take this seriously or not?" snapped Belle.

"So, let's go back to electricity," I mused. "That makes light bulbs glow, doesn't it?"

"It's that kind of in-depth technical knowledge which makes you best for lyric writing," said Maisie with some snark.

"Alright, give me a chance."

"I have an idea," said Smalt, "but it's probably no good."

"No, go on Smalt," encouraged Maisie, who always treated Smalt with respect. For this, he quietly adored her.

"There are different types of electrical current - direct current and alternating current. We call it AC and DC. Maybe we could put those letters together for a name. What about AC/DC with a slash between each group of two letters?"

"Complicated and obscure," was Whistle's objection. "Alright if our audience was a lot of sound mechanics."

"It's really good," countered Maisie, "but might be a bit too technical for our audience."

"That is very true, Miss Maisie."

"What about The Electric Light Orchestra?" chipped in Tom.

"Oh, I like that," said Maisie.

"Didn't Belle say we should get away from orchestras?" protested Whistle.

"You are good with objections," snapped Maisie. "Why not try a suggestion?"

"Well, I was thinking of Charge." He put his arms around

Belle and Long Tom each side of him, and yelled "Charge!"

CHAPTER 20

So it was I arrived back at the Coventry Road Recreation Ground, Beckenham. Eddie and Maisie were off dealing with important matters, such as devising new stage make up, hair styles and outfits. Belle, Whistle, Long Tom and Smalt had gone into the town to arrange digs for themselves and other technicians from Blackwells who would be following on. They also had to find a place to rehearse. To deal with everything else, I was left at the lodge where the park supervisor lived and where I was to have accommodation.

The man who opened the door had his natural height softened by subservience.

"Mr Tim," he said, "I am Mr Haxter."

Mr Haxter's deference was coloured, I hazarded, by a recent rise in station from local gardener to park supervisor. In a small way, he had been invited to the world of rank and now intended to make the most if it. The price of having a small team of gardeners kowtow to him was to bow and scrape to people above. This was a price Mr Haxter was willing to pay.

"The Office of the Prince of Wales, has been in touch by messenger. The communication says I am to give any help you need. I am at your service, sir."

Now, in London a young lad often finds it necessary to grow up of a sudden. One day you are playing at stall keeping, pretending some small stones are your stock, to be sold to willing customers. The next day, your old man is laid up with the bloody flux, and it's your real job to sell from the stall so you can all eat that evening. This was how it was with me now. I had never organised a concert before, only having the chaotic experience of Chatham behind me. The Good Companions had been booked ahead by Prince Edward's people. All I really did was cobble together our desperate flight to the Bull Inn. This time, according to Eddie, Prince Edward found it necessary to keep his head down after some searching questions at the Palace. So it fell to Tim to organise events. There was no escape. I took a deep breath and tried to give the impression that your narrator was a theatrical impresario of many years standing.

"Mr Haxter, by royal command there is to be a concert in your park and I am grateful for your assistance. I would appreciate a place to work, paper, nibs, ink, access to the telegraph, and a plan of the park, with entrances clearly marked. I also need an idea of how much food and drink can currently be provided by your normal vendors."

"Of course, sir. With regard to the telegraph, my gardener's boy is ready to run any communication you require to Beckenham Post Office. This is the same boy who brought a message here for you not half an hour previous. My wife will fetch this document to you. She has it in a locked pantry cupboard. Lily!"

A homely woman bustled in and gave me a bow as she handed over an envelope.

"M'lord."

Maybe my projection of false confidence had gone too far.

"Really, my good lady I'm not by any stretch of the imagination a member of the nobility."

I was opening the envelope whilst trying to deny my gentle birth, but the contents of said envelope soon put an end to diffident ramblings.

"Oh, no, no, no."

"Is there a problem, sir?" enquired Mrs Haxter.

"Eddie said a few hundred people for a few hours. That was all."

"A few hours?"

I did some forehead clutching. It seemed my clumsy efforts at concert organisation had fallen apart even at this very early stage.

"The number of people expected to attend is far larger than I anticipated."

"Would you care for some tea, m'lord? You mentioned to my husband provision of food and drink; well that's me. I supply lemonade and pastries from a small barrow near the ornamental pond."

"A small barrow?"

"Yes, sir, decorated with bunting, especially on royal holidays, or days that celebrate the victories of our glorious armed forces. Mr Haxter and myself were not blessed with children, so I think of those brave army and navy boys as our own."

"A barrow, you say? The thing is, this message says that contacts in London talk of many thousands on the way." I struck the offending telegram with the back of my hand. "They're talking of thousands of punters over two days. Struth, what about the fresh?"

"The fresh, sir?" asked Mr Haxter.

"The fresh, the sewerage, produced by thousands of people. Where do the town's people get their water?"

"Mainly from the pump in the square. Lovely, healthful water it is too, sir."

"It might not be that way much longer. Mr Haxter, if you'd be so kind as to get me a plan of the park's drainage."

"The drainage? I am a gardener primarily, not an engineer. I'll do what I can."

My inner turmoil then collided with a knock at the door, which turned out to be Eddie and Maisie. Accepting a couple of Mrs Haxter's custard pastries, without a care in the world, they proved disinterested in hearing about problems. I ushered them into the room Mr Haxter had indicated as my 'office' and shut the door.

"Just a flying visit, Tim, to see you've got the details nailed down."

"We have to stop this," I announced, waving the telegram. "No one said anything about tens of thousands of people. We've got no way to keep a handle on a crowd of that size and magnitude. Where will they all stay? How about victuals? And consider the fresh."

"What's fresh?" asked Maisie. Eddie waved the question away.

"That will all look after itself. We will make music. Everything will fall into place."

"You said a few hundred for a few hours. This will be a complete maffaking. I thought there was nothing in the papers about our Chatham concert."

"Who needs the papers? Hundreds were at the Chatham gig. They have been talking. Word has started to spread. Just have some faith, Tim. People are on the way. Some are already here." Eddie glanced through the window behind him, where indeed there was a suspiciously large number of young visitors milling about. "This is happening whether you like it or not."

"But we've still got a week to go. What are those folks doing out there?"

"They've heard rumours."

"What is fresh?" asked Maisie again.

"Some of us," pouted Eddie, "have better things to do than sit around with a negative frame of mind."

"What do you think?" I asked turning to Maisie. "You're a

genius. Can't you see this is a flummadiddle?"

Maisie, in Eddie's company was in one of her frothy moods. The proximity of Eddie appeared to suck all seriousness out of her. She made half an effort to be serious.

"I deal with the technical side," she said. "I don't know anything about concert organisation."

"I don't know anything about it either."

"You got us out of Chatham."

"Come on Maze," breezed Eddie, "let's go and look at the Beckenham boutiques."

And with that, my positive band mates left, although Maisie did cast a sympathetic glance back over her shoulder as Eddie blazed on his merry way. There seemed to be nothing for it but to try and make this work. I sank down at the desk. Mrs Haxter glanced in.

"Don't worry, dear," she counselled, "I'll make up an extra batch of pastries."

Even though it seemed that things couldn't get any worse, they soon did. Mr Haxter had answered another knock at the front door. There was a burble of conversation out in the hall, which I did not give much mind to, what with being distracted by thoughts of impending disaster.

Mr Haxter appeared in front of my desk.

"There's someone to see you, sir."

"I'm a bit busy at the moment, Mr Haxter."

The only thing I was busy at was being worried. Then the awful sound of an unwelcome voice assaulted my ears.

"Tim."

"But, what... what are you doing here?"

"Thank you, Mr Haxter. I wish to speak to the young man alone."

"Of course. If sirs will excuse me."

Mr Haxter backed out, the door closing in front of him.

"I am here with a constable, so don't even think about doing anything impetuous."

The room shrunk and shrivelled around the form of Rat and Mole Destroyer to Her Majesty, Boggo Weedy. Behind Boggo's shoulder stood a crusher in dark uniform topped by pointy helmet. Right down to his side burns, this man was very much a constable. He touched the rim of his helmet in mock salute.

"Mr Weedy. How did you find me?" I managed to wheeze.

"Never you mind about that. Let's just say a lot of people seem to be involved in your new entertainment scheme, and word got back to me. You really think you could keep this a secret?"

'Well we are preparing for it not to be a secret."

"There is much argument about all this behind the scenes. There are ramifications with the Americans."

"Are you going to arrest me?"

"I should do, boy. I should get this constable to run you down to Newgate pronto."

"But you're not going to?"

"No, I'm not. You have put me in a highly awkward position." Boggo quavered with opposing impulses, like a locomotive at full power with the brakes applied.

"I am an agent of the royal family, and I understand a member of the family is involved. As such it is my duty to protect their reputation. My sources tell me you are organising a large concert and that people are on the way. If we stop proceedings now there will be trouble. So I have a choice to make. I could go to the Queen and tell her what is going on, which will cause her much pain and upset, possibly damaging further her already strained relationship with the heir, who of course wants this concert to happen. Or I could attempt to make problems disappear before they reach Her Majesty's person. The latter course is the least worst option. I do not appreciate the position in which you leave me. When the time is right I will be getting even with you, Tim. Until then, since this concert remains under the auspices of the royal household, it will have to take place, with all the clandestine state help I can give. That means you will be moving your venue from this ridiculous little park, to a more suitable location. It has to be somewhere that is actually set up for the crowds you will get, but close to here, so that we can easily redirect those already present or on their way."

"You're going to move the concert?"

I was now the one to experience opposing impulses. Was Boggo the devil come to ruin me, or an angel sent in my hour of need? You would think it might be easy to tell these apart, since in the popular imagination they are believed to be completely different things. But no. I faced them both in the shape of Benjamin Weedy, Rat and Mole Destroyer to Her Majesty.

"Don't argue with me, boy. As the presence of crowds generates equal crowds of rats, I have experience of planning public occasions as part of my responsibilities. This place is totally inadequate. We have to move to somewhere suitable."

"Alright, if you think it best."

"What possessed you to believe a large event was possible here?"

"Foolishness."

"Utter foolishness. And if you resist my help, then I will reconsider my decision not to arrest you."

"The victory is yours, Mr Weedy. You are the better man."

Boggo puffed out his chest. But while his chest was triumphant, his eyes were hunted by the knowledge that there was trouble for him no matter which way he went with this.

"You will now relocate just a few miles away, to Penge.

I have already been in contact with the authorities at Crystal Palace and preparations are in hand."

"The Crystal Palace?"

"Yes, the Crystal Palace. They are experienced in managing large sprees."

"You mean the actual Crystal Palace?"

"From there we can control messages getting back to London afterwards, present this whole affair as some kind of experimental exhibit to demonstrate the potential of electricity in musical entertainment. But it will just be a one-off, an eccentric display, like those folding pianos or adding machines we saw at the Great Exhibition in '51. It will not be something to take seriously. That's how we'll handle it."

Boggo glared at me, his chest and eyes continuing to tell their various stories.

"You will receive help because that is demanded by a situation where we have to balance the desires of one part of the royal house against another. This does not mean you will escape the reckoning that is coming. And don't for one moment think you can talk about my intervention with anyone. If the merest breath of our conversation leaves this room, I will tell Old Ma where you are and allow her to deal out the rough justice, which you so richly deserve."

I stared at Boggo in mute astonishment. So, we were to play in a suitable location after all, and the organisation of our concert was not to rest upon my inadequate shoulders. Isn't it always this way, with good and bad luck bound up together? Those who make a living sitting in tents at fairs telling people's fortunes never inform their customers that things are so complicated. That's what I thought as Boggo made his stiff-backed exit.

CHAPTER 21

I tried to appear chipper when Eddie and Maisie returned from their shopping trip.

"I have good news."

"Well that makes a change," grumbled Eddie. "You've had the morbs ever since we got here."

"I was just concerned that this venue was not suitable. Those worries are now over because we have a new one."

"We do?" Eddie preened, appearing irritated at an imagined lack of consultation. He had this annoying way of acting as though he was above vulgar practicalities, then getting all offended if those practicalities went on without him.

"We're going to move everything to the Crystal Palace."

"The Crystal Palace?" remarked Maisie. "Is that the name of some local public house?"

"No."

"I think the Crystal Palace would be a good name for a pub. I would go there with my girlfriends. It would have big windows, fresh flowers on the table, and drinks would be served in delicate glasses. We'd only allow in pretty boys like you."

Clearly, Maisie continued in her lightness of mood.

"We are not doing a show in a girly public house," objected Eddie.

I stood up, leaning forward with my knuckles on the desk.

"There is no inn called the Crystal Palace. Well, there might be, but if there is, it has nothing to do with us."

The violence of this declaration had the desired effect. Maisie looked more like the serious girl who had invented revolutionary musical instruments.

"Alright, so where and what is this Crystal Palace?"

"It's like, you know, the actual Crystal Palace. Enormous building made of glass. Can't miss it. Used to be in Hyde Park for the Great Exhibition, but was moved to Penge. It's that Crystal Palace."

There was a brittle silence, broken by Maisie.

"The actual Crystal Palace?"

"I talked to someone who understands drainage," I said, remembering something about the best lies having some truth in them. "It was a local official. He thinks for safety reasons we should have the show there. They have space, facilities and experience. It will be perfect. They're sending some transport to help move everything."

"The actual Crystal Palace?"

"Yes, Eddie."

"The actual bleeding enormous, famous, bloody vast Crystal Palace?"

"The very same."

Maisie contributed a single, not so dignified expletive, which, as I am aiming for literature, I am not going to reproduce.

Eddie dropped his scepticism, like he was putting down a heavy bucket, which might put blisters on his soft hands.

"The Crystal Palace, Tim. I told you things would work out."

A few hours later, we left the recreation ground in Beckenham. There was a little scene of farewell as I carried my bags out of the park lodge.

"Here, m'lord, please take this as a token."

Mrs Haxter handed me a piece of her pork pie wrapped in greased paper. I had only lived with her for a few short hours, but along with doughty British boys serving in the armed forces, I had been adopted. She and Mr Haxter insisted on helping us pack our trunks in one of Eddie's carts. This would carry us a few miles over to Penge, and perhaps across the border between obscurity and fame.

CHAPTER 22

Within a half hour, I was looking up at the Crystal Palace's great glass dream, while around me the paraphernalia of an electrical musical act moved in.

"Tim," called Belle from a wide promenade running in front of the precipitous crystal frontage. "Are you alright?"

"Yes, all well."

"Venue big enough, is it?" shouted Whistle, his voice blowing in the breezy space between us.

"It should be."

"Where are you going?" yelled Belle, as though she were someone up a mountain calling to a fellow alpinist a few hundred feet below. "Come and tell us all about what's been happening."

"Can't. Have to go and see someone."

I turned to continue on my way, hearing Belle's warning shout coming after me:

"Don't ride any bicycles."

Boggo had told me where to go. Head to the building's right-hand wing, veer round the back and introduce yourself to whoever you meet there.

"Are you Mr Tim?" croaked an old, upright fella who had emerged from a humble crystalline back door, wiping his hands on an old rag. "I was told to expect ye."

"Mr Smith. I represent the entertainment company putting on the electrified musical show."

For a moment I was without any other words. I was seeing the Crystal Palace up close for the first time. Just behind Mr Smith, an endless glass facade began, or ended, in an endless reproduction of individual parts forming the vast whole of a transparent cliff face, which would challenge the describing powers of the most excitable and overblown scandal sheet in London. It was so modern in the way one piece reproduced itself in the next, on and on like a mirror reflecting into eternity. Yet this modern palace of factory repetition, reminded me of the old world, which liked nothing better than vast chateaux arranged above formal gardens of sweeping avenues, circular ponds and plashing fountains. Imagine you can see through that old world, as though a wizard had waved a wand and made gossamer all those rooms and the secrets contained therein. And after the exposed aristocrats had run away, clutching their towering hairdos and unhitched britches, maybe they would come back again with sensible hair and tidy trousers, to walk amongst admiring crowds through glass boulevards, which were inside and outside at the same time. Maybe in the future, we would live our lives in a garden where an invisible roof protected everyone from wind, rain, fear, illness and hunger. It was a happy thought going round my mind as Mr Smith conducted me through the door and led me on a tour along limpid avenues.

"I hear you planned to stage your show over at the new recreation ground at Beckenham."

"We did, but we had problems, not least with the provision of sanitation."

Mr Smith nodded in a manner suggesting he knew all about sanitation. In fact, he seemed to have an air of a man who knew everything there was to know about staging events. This was a great relief to your humble narrator.

"The Crystal Palace had the world's first public toilets. Did you know that?"

"Really, Mr Smith? That was a great achievement."

I meant it. Someone who has walked the King's Scholars' knows how much work goes into sanitation.

Mr Smith did not appear to register this praise. I felt he was a man who was always in the background looking after people, dealing with the little matter of keeping cholera and typhoid fever at bay. No one ever thanked him for saving their lives. They had other people to play hero, like Admiral Nelson, preening cove that he was, or polar explorers journeying through places no one in their right mind would ever want to go.

"So, they sent you to deal with the practicalities did they, Tim? Well, that raises you in my opinion. Men like us have to deal with practicalities, while others get on with glory and limelight. When we staged the Great Exhibition in '51, the history books make out it was a big jolly where fun was had by all. But we had some dark days back in '51. Don't be fooled by pictures of well-behaved crowds, polite in their appreciation of exhibits. There were so many people, all of them assuming that by some magic, food and drink would appear, and that their waste would be carted away so as not to give them all a little something to take home. We had to manage crowds so big that if we moved them wrong, people would be crushed to death. To break up fights, we needed constables hidden in the background, but we had to take care not to provoke fights just by having constables there. We got through, with money, hard work and luck."

Suitably pep-talked, Mr Smith showed me my office, referred to as the South Entrance Administration Area, overlooking that glorious terrace, from where Belle had recently called excited salutations. This was to be my new digs. I was to sleep in the office on a military cot brought in from Chatham.

"Is it just me in here?"

"Yes. If you are the man who has to deal with practicalities, then I will put you close to your work. The rest of your group have been placed in a guest house overlooking the park. They will be fine there."

As the first days of our residence passed, I discovered that the Crystal Palace was a very beautiful factory, making as its product events for people's amusement. In this business, it was very efficient. At the same time, I have to say there was also an air of weariness about the place, as though time had frayed the cuffs from which magic had pulled cards for so long.

At my desk, I could hear pattering water from the South Transept fountain. I sometimes walked there, to look at a quivering, liquid tower reaching up towards a ceiling of repeating panes of glass, stretching across a blue sky. When this place was first built, walking in here must have been like finding yourself in tomorrow. Now I could see a layer of dust and the odd splurge of mossy mould staining heaven's glassy vault. The sun was bright and perfect this morning. Mornings as bright and unblemished as this one must also have dawned over the world a million years ago. There's nothing like sunlight to show up dusty glass, reminding us that we haven't quite worked out that trick perfected by the sun, of repeating things like they were new, every day, for aeons.

Our stage was arranged on the terrace, backed by that great, crystal wall, which during the performance, would be lit by an arrangement of changing coloured lights. As for the sound aspect, steam powered generators had increased in their power since Chatham. Those engines drove electrical noise boxes piled up each side of the stage, and placed upon wooden latticed towers.

Once Blackwell's men had set up all this machine wonder, rehearsals started. On that first day, I was standing on the stage wings surrounded by electrical music. Whistle was playing a solo from a song I had called Comfortably Benumbed, inspired by the experience of taking an apothecary item during my recovery from my bumped head. Whistle's guitar was soaring, like all the yearning you ever done packed into a song. He had this way of raking into phrases, which had the effect of squeezing excitement from every note. There was repetition and development, a sense of music shaped, even as he found his way from one spontaneous moment to the next. Then after pulling every emotion of human longing from metal strings and electricity, he jumped up an octave, and, oh my heart, did it again.

I had written our words, listened to our band from its beginnings, but struggled to believe what we had become. It was as though my life before the disaster of Victoria's ring had been one of comfortable numbness. But that guitar, so yearning and painful, had ruined my old existence. Even if by some miracle Old Ma ever forgave me for what I did with Queen Victoria's ring, I could never go back. From the moment Maisie played her first volcanic guitar chord at Rules, the comfort of my old days had blown away.

I reeled up a sweep of wide steps, heading towards the South Entrance office.

"Was it alright?" called Whistle from the stage.

"Yes," I manage to choke.

"We're still working on the sustain. It's different to a normal guitar."

Only a nod was possible before I walked through the crystal gateway and sought out the reassuring human scale of my office.

Mr Smith was sitting in there waiting for me, his face showing an unfamiliar greyness.

"Mr Smith?"

"Sit down, lad."

I did as asked, uneasiness joining the turmoil of my feelings.

"We deal in concerts all the time. When they told us we would have to work with you, I thought it was just another job. But this... I've never heard anything like it."

"Things are only new for a while, Mr Smith. We'll get used to it."

"I saw lots of new things at the exhibition back in '51. But when you look with your eyes at something extraordinary, the wonder stays outside you. When you hear something extraordinary, then it's different. It gets inside. This music has got into my head."

"I know it's a shock."

Mr Smith was too distressed to continue sitting. He got up and walked about, appearing incapable of remaining still under the dominion of such sound. Maisie's base notes were soft concussions through the office, while Whistle's guitar soared overhead.

"I think if I didn't have certain very important people telling me to help you with this concert, I would be throwing you youngsters out on your ear."

Mr Smith took time out from his office ramblings to beat his fist on the desk to emphasise his last words.

"Another part of me wants to clap you on the back, and I am not a man known for emotional displays. Just ask Mrs Smith. What are you doing? Have you asked yourself that? If your music provokes turmoil in me, a man who enjoys the benefits of a lifetime of steady employment, and a personality confined to the practical, how are the young people going to feel? Have you thought about what might happen when you unleash this music on the susceptible?"

"I have just been thinking about my lyrics, Rawbone."

"Rawbone?"

"Rawbone?"

"That's what you called me."

"Sorry, did I? He's someone I used to know."

I looked at Mr Smith who had become a replacement

Rawbone for me. I was in such a strange and unexpected situation, that it seems I had taken someone from my old life and tried to find him in this new one.

"Rawbone was a dear old fella - tosher, waterman, philosopher and pearly king. He knew everything there was to know about the dodges of finding. To support my writing career, I sometimes did some toshing. Anyone who is experienced in any of the finding trades knows how messy and careless people are. We made our living out of that. There was a fair amount of money flowing into Blue Anchor Yard, which went some way to Rawbone being able to help me afford an education. But toshing won't last. I see that now. A few more years and there won't be a trade anymore. The people I lived with didn't want to face up to that painful fact. Like a fool, I tried to help with a crazy plan to find Queen Victoria's ring in the sewers. But there is nothing we can do to stop things changing."

There was silence after this outburst, which had been building up within me for the longest time. Mr Smith clearly didn't like so many words. Yet he hung on each one, like a man clinging to a broken spar following a shipwreck.

"All I'll say to you, Tim, is good luck. I will do whatever I can to help."

CHAPTER 23

After a few days of emotionally overwhelming music and busy organisational work with Mr Smith, I felt a need for stillness. There was a palm-fringed oasis up on one of those long balconies, running behind the crystal facade. During a break in rehearsals, I sought out this sanctuary, sitting grateful and quiet at a table inlaid with a white and grey arabesque terracotta mosaic. My chair, forged in swirling, black wrought iron, had a matching mosaic panel on its backrest.

This might have been a roof garden somewhere down Algiers way, except for the fact that we were only about eight miles from Rosemary Lane and the blue sky above me was made of glass. Looking up at that glassy heaven, blurred patches of rain-washed dust, and blooms of moss were again evident. My mind wandered. Imagine if the sky really did wear out. Imagine it would wear out in, say, five years. Then I would look at everything about me and it would all be valuable, every last thing.

Back in '51 these glass galleries had been filled with arts and manufactories from the world over, as though collected in a glass ark. Since then, after moving to Penge, the Crystal Palace had staged aeronautic exhibitions, art displays, concerts, and the world's first event for people to show off their cats. Cats, music, machines to make drinks and ices, devices to iron clothes. If the world were only to last another five years, everything would be valuable. Gather everything in a vast, crystal warehouse and keep it safe.

Upon paper softened by palm frond shade, I was busting

myself up to write a song about all this, when a person-shaped shadow fell across the table. My eye passed through a dark smudge, and rose to meet Boggo.

Without invitation, Boggo sat himself down in the empty chair opposite mine. He did not look his best. His clothing, which usually rejected any association with the practical business of chasing of rats and moles, had now begun to look as though some rat and mole chasing might have recently occurred. The vinegar smell of alcohol hung about him. He was of a sudden a man giving every impression of someone brought low. Perhaps it is the most upstanding who catch the wind most directly and have the harder smash.

"Mr Weedy, what are you doing here?"

"We have to talk."

"But I thought we agreed....You said yourself, there are powerful people who want this concert to happen."

"Ah yes, your powerful friends. That would be Prince Edward and a girl who invents things. Those are your connections. A prince whose actions endlessly disappoint and an eccentric young woman. But I've already told you that I am obliged to support this concert and will do so. Believe or not my intentions are honourable."

"So what is it I can do for you? Perhaps you would like to speak to Mr Smith. I am but his humble assistant."

"Never mind about Smith. It's the music I'm here to talk to you about. I watched a rehearsal this afternoon. After seeing it, I am worried. I have to ask for your... help."

That last word didn't come out without the sort of effort that an old sailor might put into a cough.

"My help?"

"Yes. From what I heard, this music could be a spark to a bag of gunpowder."

"I'm sure it'll be alright. It's just singing and musical

accompaniment with some electrical amplification."

"But it's not just that, is it? Don't you realise that music is like a violent man who has to be trained into decency? Music has to be beaten down with bow ties and evening dress, or a military uniform. I know this, because..."

I was surprised that Boggo had such strong opinions about music.

"I don't understand."

"You know they call him Edward the Caresser, don't you?"

"Who, Prince Edward? I..."

Was it best to admit my knowledge of the princely nickname, or show ignorance of something I knew a royal servant would not approve of? My compromise between these two options came out as a kind of spluttering, which Boggo ignored.

"Like a fool, I thought it was alright. If he could behave in a certain manner, a member of the royal family, how could it be so wrong to have affairs with women other than your wife?"

Boggo's voice cracked on the word wife, as though a wife was an object of beautiful cut glass, which he had just at that moment, dropped.

"I carried on with another woman. There I said it. For a long time I have swanked about the place as though I'm a man of the world. But it's a lie. So, I have come here to tell you what I have done."

"Mr Weedy, that really isn't necessary..."

"It is necessary, and don't you get out of that seat. Her name was Maria. She played the violin, not in a Royal Opera House way, but with wide, sweeping emotion, her blue eyes looking inward, her stance always appearing to move forward even as she stayed in one place. It was at a Shoreditch inn. She was playing Irish reels. The music seemed to set something free in me. And there I was thinking that Prince Edward was doing whatever he liked.

He was heir to the throne, his behaviour an example for the rest of us. Two things made me weak that night, the two things that I blame for ruining my life - Prince Edward for his poor example and music which brought out the beast in me."

Boggo paused to catch his breath. I apprised him with some level of horror, wondering what I was to do, and also aghast that a lively fiddler woman would be accepting of Boggo's advances.

"Please, Mr Weedy, you might want to keep your voice down if you wish for this information to remain discreet."

Boggo continued with no appreciable lessening of volume. He appeared beyond caring. Fortunately for him no one was near enough to hear his royal heresy.

"I went with a woman who was not my wife. When my wife found out about it, that was the end of my marriage. She didn't accept my behaviour, as Alexandra of Denmark would have done - the poor woman who has the misfortune to be married to Prince Edward. I just worked in the Prince's world, a servant to it. I was in it but not of it."

Boggo placed his elbows on the table, plunging his face into a cradle of his hands. There his face stayed for a few moments, before the broken visage rose to address me once again.

"I have tried to deny the dark side of my life, tried to be a big gentleman. Of late it has become insupportable. I know what you all think of me, a jumped up coster, who is against you. The truth is I tried to help, tried to get toshers out of the sewers and costers into regulated markets. But those people don't want to be helped. They cling to their miserable lives and treat me like a villain."

Of a sudden, I felt sorry for Boggo. There had been a side of him, buried deep in self-importance, which had been sincere in efforts to do good.

"I think maybe they just felt you were trying to take their livelihoods."

"If people want to continue in livelihoods that kill them, then there's nothing that can be done about it. Today we have more pressing concerns."

"We do?"

"I was ruined by the Prince of Wales, and by music. You see, the Prince is the lesser of these two problems. His behaviour is disguised by people who have long experience of shady work. For this reason, Prince Edward's moral turpitude will not diminish the world at large. But your rehearsal... although His Highnesses failings can be hidden, this music is a beast that will not be contained. It already jumps over the walls of Crystal Palace Gardens and has people talking. It is a beast I tell you, a threat to social coherence, which will jolt people out of their places. Bells of Hell? What is the Church of England going to say about that? Are you completely mad? Big Ben, standing proud above the mother of parliaments, is not the bell of hell. It's unacceptable to mention Big Ben and hell in the same sentence."

I had no idea what to say to this outpouring, merely staring at Boggo in a bewilderment that mirrored his own. Maybe he took this as an expression of sympathy, because his tone now softened a tad.

"I said before that I will help this concert go ahead because, God help me, that is my only choice. Thousands of people are coming and the quietest way to get rid of them is to give them a portion of what they want. Once this concert is over, plans are already in place for appropriate authorities to remind Prince Edward as to the nature of his constitutional responsibilities. But before that happens I need your... help."

"My help."

I searched the situation for any possible way in which a young London lad, surviving on hope and Crystal Palace savouries, provided gratis by Mr Smith, could help a royal appointed Rat and Mole Destroyer.

"I really don't see how I can assist, Mr Weedy. What is it that you needs help with exactly?"

"I had a daughter with Maria - Isabelle, the young lady you call Belle. I want you to protect her."

I sat staggered in my chair. What was this world I had fallen into, with Maisie and Eddie possibly son and daughter of Prince Edward, and now Belle the daughter of Boggo? It was a place of chaos, full of hidden links which made me think of Long Tom's drumming, full of disciplined patterns that kept darting away as you tried to hold them in your head.

"Isabelle has taken after Maria. She has the same musical skill. I have sat in a corner of the park during your rehearsals, and I can appreciate her abilities. I can appreciate the abilities of all of you. But I tell you this, Tim, your talent has been corrupted. You will turn people's minds. This is not music, this is revolution."

Boggo leant back in his wrought iron chair, two front legs lifting off the balcony. Leaves hanging from an indoor tree near my table moved with tiny motion. I'd have failed to notice this in any other moment. You wouldn't have thought there could be a wind indoors, but Mr Smith had told me about Joseph Paxton's ventilation system. Movable glass panels allowed warm air to flow outwards, creating a lower pressure within the building, which drew cooler air in through narrow gaps between all the floorboards. This system was one of many matters Mr Smith explained to me. Following Boggo's revelation, the only thing I could focus on were those leaves going through their tiny cycles in the Crystal Palace's own weather.

"I have tried to help Isabelle over the years. As Rat and Mole Destroyer to Her Majesty, I was in a position to introduce Isabelle to a number of eligible young men, all with good prospects in public sanitation. But like you people, she threw my efforts back in my face. She took her mother's name, Rafferty. Now, she has fallen in with these electric musicians."

Boggo paused for some running of hands through greasy

hair.

"There's the Prince on one side and the Queen on the other, with my daughter in-between. I have to look after the reputations of them all, by doing things that one or more of them will hate me for and for which I will hate myself."

Boggo glared at me. His eyes then seemed to search the mosaic tabletop for a drink that wasn't there.

"You're a clever boy and a fellow graduate of Almanac's chambers. Isabelle won't let me help directly, so I am asking you to look out for her."

"Look out for her? What can I do? She's really the one who looks out for me."

"Don't be ridiculous."

With a sharp scraping of metal upon metal, Boggo pushed his chair backwards and stood up. A shattered Rat and Mole Destroyer stalked off, weighed down forwards like a ship with flooding below decks. As he moved away, parallel lines of glass and metal perspective shrunk him down until he sank through the floor, via a staircase leading to the main atrium.

"Alright there?" shouted Mr Smith from below, as he did the rounds of his beloved Crystal Palace.

"All's well," came my quavering and not convincing reply. Mr Smith looked up at me with worry on his face, the anxiety of a settled man facing change. He walked on, continuing his endless mission to make sure his Crystal Place stood forever.

CHAPTER 24

The day of the concert arrived. Waking after a few hours' sleep, the windowpanes in my glass-walled room now presented themselves as the same dark night painted over and over by an obsessive artist. I breakfasted on cheese and bread, after which our resident compulsive artist began to work on endless studies of grey dawn. I wondered if Mr Smith had been to bed when he shuffled into the South Entrance office just after half past five. We greeted each other with a nod that let gravity do most of the work.

"We've done this many times," he said, talking to himself as much as to me. "It's like the Handel Festival, but bigger."

"This crowd won't be like the one for Handel. It will be more like the one that goes to see horse racing, or watches the Royal Arsenal at Plumstead. People will be moving around, shouting, jumping up and down."

"Aye. There will be those in high places who won't like it. Governments prefer people to keep still."

"That they do, Mr Smith."

"But I have been looking after visitors for a long time. Not all of them have been well behaved. We know what we're doing. Once again I thank the fates that you came to us and didn't try this in your Beckenham park."

Over the space of a silent moment, I, in an inward manner, gave the same thanks.

"My staff tell me that queues are already building at the gates. We will open 11am, prompt."

I already knew when the gates would open, but it made us both feel more in control to state obvious things about the schedule. This same sentiment also lay behind Mr Smith describing our jobs for the day, even though the plan was already familiar.

"I will be out and about tending to matters as they come up. You'll be here, close to the stage and deal with that end of things."

"Good luck, Mr Smith."

"Good luck, Tim. God help us."

Mr Smith walked off into brightening sunlight.

You spend far more time preparing for something than you do experiencing it. The day itself, when it comes, is a distillation of all the days you have laboured through in a monotonous sequence of trying and trying again. Judgement day is a concentration of normal days. If your normal days had a little piece of progress in them, then there is a chance you will jump forward when judgement arrives. If you slipped back with each passing dawn, then there comes a morning when the ground might open up beneath your feet. You never know until the time comes. After all, life isn't always fair in the rewards and punishments it deals out. One thing is clear - on the day, whether your fate is success or failure, it is too late now to influence the outcome. All you can do is hope.

Fortunately for us, Mr Smith's Crystal Palace organisation was working well, even if he did not really take my advice about preparing for a sports rather than a music event. There was a flurry of panic when chairs laid out in arcs on the lawns failed to remain in their neat lines. With this rearranging complete, the crowd enjoyed the daytime hours as a kind of carnival, not all that different to jamborees I had experienced in London. But when it got dark, the entire atmosphere became exaggerated. The Crystal Palace was now a checkerboard of coloured, electrical illumination. Red and white flares brightened the crowd areas, creating regions of luminous heaven and conflagrant hell, both packed with people, variously saved and damned, moving from one to the other. Infernal flare smoke rendered the beam from an electrical Blackwell lamp into a solid column of angelic light, which you might almost climb up inside, upon Jacob's Ladder.

And so, after singalongs, sword swallowings, jugglers, brass bands from Fulham, music hall singers from the Wilton, magicians and fiddle players from Ireland, Eddie walked out upon the stage, his face a painted mirage. A glittering, scarlet lightning bolt shot across pale forehead, continuing on down past right eye, flashing up across left eye and then falling again across opposite cheek. No longer was it possible to dismiss all that time Eddie and Maisie had dedicated to make-up and costume. Judgement passed its positive verdict on their efforts.

I didn't so much hear the crowd as feel it, a profound force that usually scattered itself about the place, along pavements, shouting the name of a scandal sheet, calling out for rags and bones, in shops asking for a pound of sausage, nattering in houses over a glass of port and asking for salt to be passed. All of those voices and countless others, now came together with one overwhelming vigour. And it was not as though most of them knew what it was they were getting excited about. There was a noisy group from Chatham who had already seen us, including the fellow who got us out of the Jolly Companions. I did promise him a ticket after all. But there were so many people who were not from Chatham, who had never seen us and were excited by rumour and whisper, which maybe explains their ferment. Rumour in Blue Anchor Yard passes from mouth to mouth like a secret, a secret everyone thinks they are in on, which continues to tease in the way you're not sure of facts. Rumour facts are more interesting than normal, real facts, because they can twist and change and develop according to personal requirements, seeming to belong specially to you and your kin alone.

I wondered at Eddie's bravery going out there, as you might

admire the bravery of a man going over Niagara's thunderous falls in a barrel. He had his hand above his head in greeting, or maybe to shade his eyes from Blackwell's lamp.

"Good evening, everyone. Are we all ready?"

A great roar, indicated that yes we were all ready.

"Let me introduce the greatest rock and roll band in the world - the only rock and roll band in the world - Charge!"

Rock and roll? Had Eddie just made that phrase up to describe our turbulent music? Recalling Boggo's demand that I keep his daughter safe, I asked myself how it was possible for little me to do that, when the world rocked and rolled beneath our feet like an earthquake. Of all the people he could have asked - a burly Guards officer, a hired heavy - he chose me. But of course if this whole thing went sour, nothing could be done to save Belle, or any of us. In this fearful state of mind, I watched Eddie waving at the audience.

Long Tom was the first to follow Eddie out there, like it was every night he went under blinding, voltaic lights and the weight of such noise. He climbed up behind his drums, sitting safe and secure, a lord in his castle. As for Whistle, the illumination tore away all the shady excuses used to explain his lack of success. No more moaning that the world wasn't ready for his music. He had his music to give and an audience waiting for it, like hungry people anticipating food. There was a look of terror on his face.

"I don't think I can do this."

"Just get your backside out there," was Belle's advice. "If you don't, you and me is finished."

"Alright. Hell's teeth. Give me a second."

Belle barged with a shoulder, Whistle falling forward into the bright void, his hands outstretched, the initial real stumble complemented by a second pretend lurch and some apparently drunken steps, all designed to lend a little knockabout humour.

He was a professional when it reached the crunch.

That left only the girls to take the stage. Maisie came to stand beside Belle. They made final adjustments to their electrical instruments.

"Are you ready?" asked Maisie of her friend.

"I am, dearie."

It didn't matter that Belle's answer was drowned out and inaudible. I heard what she said in the same way as Maisie, by following the movement of lips. I could see that Belle's message came through like a calm voice on a still evening. Arm in arm they went into the dreadful cockpit.

Big Ben's tolls of past time, resurrected by Smalt's electrical second coming, boomed across Crystal Palace Park. I felt a lurching of worlds as the crowd roared. Their many-pitched clamour was a match for Maisie's noise engines, as though the sound these people wanted to hear lay within them, as well as pummelling them from without. All those people were part of it. They witnessed, and they created.

Eddie pouted and vamped his way through Bells of Hell. I feared the crowd would go mad, but our music releasing their pent up energy, also provided somewhere for it to go. Lightning was its own lightning rod, striking many times atop a silhouetted church tower as the heavens roiled.

It was hard to tell when one song ended and another began. The night seemed to rise above such fake categories. Eddie started to sing the dude song, picking out individuals just as he'd done in Chatham. The people he chose were grateful for it, but equally grateful to fall back as a cog in something turning.

Eddie sang our song about fashion, before taking it all back home with Music Hall Woman. I closed my eyes and stood again in the Wilton cellar. Long Tom was still going round and round in that circular rhythm, which even now continued to dart away from my ears. Whistle's guitar line bent and weaved its way around a sense of insistent progress. After Music Hall Woman, Eddie quietened things down with the beginning of Edward's song about kings and queens. This calmness was only a coaching inn on a longer journey, gathering energy and passion, building to that one day, a day like this, when we could all be kings and queens. That led straight into Captain Tim's Odd Odyssey, followed by Comfortably Benumbed, Whistle's guitar yearning upward ever higher, making me wonder how high the top of topper-most could ever be.

Finally, there did have to be an end. We had a number of false endings, a reprise of the dude song, followed by a triumphant encore of Bells of Hell, as though everything was starting again from the very beginning. Even then there had to be an end. And so it came, with a song we had written about an outdoor concert, a festival of music, which people could attend without monetary payment. Eddie sang soaring sentiments about travellers from beyond this world coming to listen. He seemed to paint my word pictures on white balloons, which he sent flying over a tumult of heads and raised arms. I know all this sounds enthuzimuzzy, as the costers used to say back in Rosemary Lane, if someone got carried away with their patter. I would answer that occasionally things are not Earth bound. This was one of those times. It seemed as if the very essence of joy ran through Crystal Palace Park. It didn't really I suppose, but the lack of factual joy became this rumour of joy, passing between audience and musicians, growing even more powerful as a result. I sang along with a chorus I had written to the clever ones who had made our noise and light machines.

I think only that song could have saved us, bringing the crowd home in a way that allowed them to give up this completeness they had together, before walking out into Penge, back to their lives, unchained, as small parts of the whole they had once been.

CHAPTER 25

The following evening, back in London, we regrouped at Rules in a piecemeal kind of way. Everybody was there, musicians, technicians, sponsors. I arrived to the sound of levity and compared experiences. People wandered about with food in their hands, enjoying an event that was part meal, part business meeting, part social occasion. This manner of eating is called a buffet, which is truly a meal for the new age. I had always thought of meals as natural breaks during the day, a time when you stopped and sat down. Now we kept on moving, plate and fork in hand.

I took a bite of pork pie, enjoying my sense of relief that we had lived through a trial and come out triumphant. You'd think in a story there would now be a rest, a pause in proceedings to catch your breath. Once again, my life fell awkwardly for someone who has to try to put it on paper. You can understand my dismay when, drifting around our Rules stand-up supper, I started hearing the words 'Hyde Park gig' coming from various quarters.

I went to the food table and found myself standing beside Long Tom. He was stocking his plate with ham and small cakes. First and second course were as one.

"What's going on?" I asked in an undertone.

"I is just getting some food."

"Yes, I can see that."

"There's a quail pie over there. Luverly it is. Get over there before the quality take it all."

"Never mind about the food. What's the bobbins about Hyde Park?"

"I dunno. Something about the next gig, maybe."

"Another gig? But we have only just done one. Lordy."

"Go talk to Belle. She'll know."

Before I could find Belle, Whistle slapped me with force around the shoulders.

"Timmy, man."

"How are you?"

"Bloody brilliant is how I am."

Whistle was all shining eyes and unnatural energy.

"Have you had some sleep?" I enquired.

It was as though Whistle had been shaken out of normal life - that kind of existence where people get up, attend work, return home, have supper and retire to a welcome bed in a regular manner, so as they can get through the years without wearing themselves out too early on. Knocked from this pattern, Whistle was spinning like a top whipped along a pavement.

"You should have got some rest."

"No time for that."

"How are you still awake?"

"A mate of the Prince sorted me out."

I did not want details. I knew this sort of thing went on amongst the creative crowd. Need I remind you of Balzac sticking his head in a barrel of rotten apples? This new music was mightily exciting, but was also hard, demanding work. If your employment is demanding work, it does not pay to throw everything over and stay up for nights on end.

"Where's Belle?"

Whistle's hectic eyes flashed towards the kitchen doors. Belle was beside them, in conference with Eddie and Maisie.

"You take care, Whistle. Get some sleep."

"Yes, thanks for the advice, Rawbone."

Ignoring Whistle's gibes, I made a slow approach to a tight huddle of conversation. Belle was the first to notice me.

"Timmy, luv, we were just talking about you."

"Oh, you were?"

"Just wondering if you had any more songs on the way."

"I have some ideas. Why do you ask?"

"For the Hyde Park gig."

"Hyde Park? But we've only just survived Crystal Palace."

"We have to keep things moving along," opined Belle. "We aim to make a real splash in London and then start selling records and record players."

"We have to wait for the Prince," cautioned Maisie. "I get the feeling something is going on."

"Going on, like what?"

"I'm not sure yet. I expect it will involve money, as usual."

Before Belle could ask any more questions, there was action at the doors, involving formal bowing combined with bonhomie. It was Prince Edward radiating a measure of friendship and good humour, though in a rather more subdued manner than usual. Beside him was an individual I judged to be the dampening influence on his mood. I'd never seen him before. His haughty carriage suggested drink and gambling, in their socially respectable forms. Drink was taken with well-connected friends in the smartest clubs, while gambling was a matter of horses running at only the most genteel race meetings, or cards among gentlemen where the worst crime would be failure to honour debt.

There were handshakes and a call for drinks all round. Something wasn't right. Prince Edward usually leant forward into a handshake. Today he did not leave the vertical. While his smile was as warm as ever, it was framed by wintery crinkles.

"What's the matter with Edward?" I asked this question more to myself than anyone. But at that particular moment, it was Long Tom who was close enough to hear it.

"Dunno."

"Something's out of kilter."

Before I could make any more enquiries, the sound of silver spoon tinkling against glass, cut through the buzz of conversation.

"Everyone," declaimed Edward. "If I could just get your attention. Thank you. Thank you. Heartiest congratulations are in order for the marvellous show at Crystal Palace. It was a thrilling and ground-breaking event which I will never forget even if I live and reign as long as my mother."

This was answered with a manner of laughter, which comes from people who feel themselves at the centre of things.

"First triumph of many," shouted a voice, which was definitely a woman's and may have belonged to Belle.

A blast of cold weather around the eyes accompanied Edward's continuing efforts to maintain his smile.

"Ah yes. I know many of you must be thinking about the future. This music, after all, is the sound of the future. With that in mind, what you are about to hear may disappoint. It would probably be easier if I now hand over to Mr Carlton."

Now we knew - Prince Edwards' companion was a Mr Carlton, a man who appeared happy, nay honoured, to be chosen as the bearer of bad news. Some people make hard decisions because they have to. I was quick to decide that this man sought out hard judgements, because it made him feel big to dish out unpleasant consequences to those on the downside of a determination.

"Good evening, ladies and gentleman. I hear congratulations are in order with regard to your recent concert.

Well done, well done, all. I hope you will be proud of what you have achieved under Prince Edward's patronage."

This was greeted with some half-hearted cheers, from those desperate to hang on to the golden feelings that had brightened this room before Carlton arrived. No cheers emanated from me. I wasn't a big public speaker, but even I knew that a speech of commendation, builds up to final applause. If that applause comes too soon, then there is a codicil coming, which is going to take the shine off.

"The Prince", continued Carlton, "is pleased and honoured to have been part of your efforts. It is his sincere hope that the work you have done together will lead on towards exciting future developments. For that to happen there will need to be a change of course. I am sure you are all aware that a man in the Prince's position has to make decisions with regard to a wide set of contingencies. Although His Royal Highness's involvement in this musical project has to end, he looks forward to the application of the technical advances you have developed in other areas. Don't look at this as an ending, but as a new beginning, for both yourselves and our great country."

Our great country - when people say that, it always means trouble.

"Who is this man?" asked Eddie in an undertone.

"I don't know."

"What's he saying, exactly?" I asked.

"I'm not sure, but I think…"

Prince Edward stepped forward once again, interrupting Eddie's unfinished opinion.

"I am so sorry. We owe it to you to be frank." A glance of distaste flashed from Edward's eyes towards Carlton. "For various reasons, the musical aspect of our collaboration must come to an end. It is not my wish, but it seems I am obligated to ask that your work now takes a different direction."

"What direction is that?" called a voice.

"The military direction," declared Carlton.

There was a uniform mass intake of breath, followed by all kinds of scatted exhalations of shock.

Prince Edward tossed a chilly smile towards us, like a bitter gaming chip cast aside following an unsuccessful bet on a Mayfair card table.

"I'd love to continue my involvement. You are great people and the concert was an absolute triumph. However, we are a victim of our own success. Questions are being asked at the highest levels. Despite our efforts to control the news, we might not be able to manage some elements of Fleet Street if this goes on much longer. There are those in government who fear large scale social disturbance."

"There was no disturbance," objected Belle. "Well, not in a bad way. It was a good disturbance."

"As far as the government is concerned," answered Prince Edward, "there is no good disturbance, except perhaps for that of our servicemen letting off steam in Chatham. What we had at Crystal Palace was different. It did not involve soldiers in a military town, but ordinary people in a place where an audience in evening dress usually listens to Handel. H.M. Government don't like it. I know these government fellows. I have seen them close up, both drunk and sober. Believe me, they do not take kindly to any form of violent ecstasy, unless it's off-duty military relaxation. I'm sorry, but Mama is getting on now. There are officials saying I have to behave, because, you know, at some point the throne beckons. So, we have to stop this. Maisie can continue her work, but she has to do so through different channels."

Carlton turned to Maisie.

"Miss Gladwish, I have arranged for someone at the War Office to contact you. H.M. Government will see that you have every facility. They would like you to work on military communications systems and airships."

"Airships," mused Whistle. "That might not be so bad."

"Shut it, Whistle," snapped Belle.

"This really is the best way for Miss Gladwish to continue her work," pontificated Carlton. "Maybe we could find something for the rest of you to do. The engineers can continue to assist Miss Gladwish with technical projects. As for you musicians, there's clerical work perhaps?"

I glanced at Prince Edward to see how he was taking this. It was unsettling to see a glistening in eyes not meant for sadness. He now spoke words that made me think on a winter pond, covered in smooth ice, which might break under the weight of any careless skater.

"Working with you musicians has been the most exciting time of my life. I can't tell you... Our song about all of us waiting to be kings and queens; that was wonderful. You see, the music isn't the problem. The world is the problem. It just isn't ready, and may not be ready for a long time. We can only console ourselves that perhaps the children of our children's children will enjoy the excitement, which we have tasted so briefly. It has been decided that all work on electric music will cease. Friends in Fleet Street will be fed a line that our Crystal Palace concert involved the demonstration of new but impractical audio machinery. We just have to walk away."

Eddie turned to Maisie.

"Did you get all of that?"

"I got enough. A little of that is too much."

Maisie looked away from Eddie, turning her attention downwards towards an odd sketch that she was shaping on a napkin. I guessed the pencil in her hand, had in happier moments, created designs for noise machines. Craning to get a better look, I realised the drawing caught a terrible moment in Carlton's version of her future. A scatter of tiny buildings lined the page's bottom edge, all serving to accent the heaven-reaching zenith of an Eiffel Tower-like structure, and the vast bulk of an airship beside it. I assumed the tower represented a vertical quayside standing out into atmospheric oceans, waiting for airships to make safe landfall. But there had been a disaster. Nose up, the rear half ablaze, charcoal pencil flames at the pointy bow suggested an all-encompassing interior paroxysm. This ship was doomed.

Carlton addressed the aghast assembly.

"Come, come, I know the music was fun, but in the end, Miss Gladwish's work is far too important to waste on mere entertainment."

I think Maisie registered this, since she happened to be looking at Carlton as these words left that man's self-satisfied lips.

"We can't just let this go," shouted a voice.

Eddie answered for most of us:

"What can we do against the government?"

"The government are against lots of things," objected Whistle. "That doesn't mean they don't happen."

"Like what?" asked Carlton, taken aback by such an outlandish idea.

"Like, oh I don't know... bookies. There are laws against bookies, but there are still thousands of them."

"Well said," chortled Prince Edward, before stifling his reaction in response to a supercilious glance from Carlton.

"Look," said Belle, "if you think I am going to give up electrified guitar and go back to playing fiddle in some operetta at Norwich Playhouse, you can forget it."

At this point Belle put her arm around me. Until now, I would have bowed to judgement that our musical project had been fun while it lasted. But Belle had put her arm around me. I couldn't let her down. She had bathed my cycling wounds.

"Belle's right," I piped up. "We have combined modish science with an ancient musical inheritance coming to us from Africa through the docks of London. We have taken science and filled it with humanity. That is a much better way to use ground-breaking knowledge than sending it to the War Office."

Maisie seemed to approve of my little speech. Her arm joined Belle's around my shoulders. At that moment I would have faced up to mounted troops.

"Yes, fine words," gloated Carlton. "But this is about realities. Isn't that right, Your Highness?"

Prince Edward faced back at Carlton, maybe wishing that this man who liked cards and horse race meetings, was more of an actual risk-taker, rather than a man whose risk-taking only extended to showing off an exalted social station. The royal gaze turned to me.

"Your words touch me, young man. As I say, working with you all has been the honour of my life. But the fact remains I am not able to support a continuation of this project. I wish it were different."

Prince Edward had nothing to offer now but regret. I supposed Maisie would be compelled to work for the state. If she resisted, they could easily make trouble for her. And while Maisie disappeared into a government laboratory, what of the rest of us? If this office filing work was really on offer, then I doubt anyone would accept it. Despite her protestations, Belle would probably go back to playing fiddle in a playhouse somewhere. Eddie might work in music hall. Long Tom would be obliged to resign himself to working for Enfield, while on occasion banging a single, solitary drum in a pearly parade. And Whistle - now he was the one I wondered about the most. Perhaps for him the end of this journey would be the deepest cut of all, with his insecurities, his weakness for alcohol and opium-eating, and his great skill for a style of music he could not play to anyone anymore. Another contrary part of me thought that maybe the end coming now would be best for him. There was monstrous success lurking in this music. I could imagine worship for its practitioners, transfigured into gods upon Earth. Whistle, for one, was not a man who would live sensibly with such a consummation. Whistle had endured years of frustration, without coming to much harm. Ascendency, however, might very well be the finish of him.

So the end had come, the end of something that we all felt had not been followed to its completion. I looked again at Maisie's doomed ship of the air, the charcoal in her hand seemingly the cold embers of those fires she depicted. While a small part of me felt relief that my life would not now change out of all recognition, this reprieve was a flammable vapour set alight by disappointment, my soul falling like a flaming sky vessel.

Only in books does some kind of guardian angel come along to save you at the last. And even in books, a guardian angel arriving twice is stretching it. You could say what happened next was an angel come to save us, but if you do it's you writing the book, not me.

Anyhow, there was another fuss at the door. The previous commotion with Edward's arrival had been an effort to draw something in, the doormen comporting themselves like polite fishermen trying to make a catch with manners and etiquette. This time was different. Have you ever seen a bunch of hoods surrounding a mark on the street, attempting to hustle him into a carriage in such a way that passers-by would not realise there was anything untoward going on? Was there a scuffle or wasn't there? Were bow ties askew?

"Oh no," cried Belle.

Maisie's arm quit my shoulder.

"What's going on?" demanded Eddie, now standing and

looking.

"Oh no," repeated Belle.

"It's that awful rat and mole man," remarked Prince Edward. "My God, I think he's drunk. Allow him through. Let's see what he wants."

So no guardian angel then, just the royal rodent catcher who had turned up last time I needed divine intervention. Shrugging off the huddle of Rules staff, Boggo swayed towards us. I glanced at Prince Edward, a man whose habitual floridness at the pale roots of his beard, suggested a liking for drink - but never in sadness. Perhaps it was the way Boggo came over as a sad drunk that really caused offence.

The Royal Rat and Mole Destroyer continued his unsteady approach, stopping a wary six feet or so from our group.

"Isabelle, you need to come home with me. It is not safe to stay with these people."

"These people?" objected Carlton. "One of them is heir to the throne."

"Makes no difference."

"In all normal circumstances," pontificated Prince Edward, "I would be the first to support the normal chain of command vis-à-vis father and daughter. But I'm sorry, Weedy, you're just going to have to let Belle get on with her life. She's an incredibly talented young lady."

Boggo shook in his efforts to remain still.

"Whom is it that I serve?" asked Boggo.

"I beg your pardon?" replied Prince Edward.

"Your mother is the reigning Queen. You are heir to the throne. Whom is it that I serve?"

"We all serve the Queen."

"Are you serving the Queen with your actions?"

"You are talking of matters that are above your station."

"Am I?"

Boggo dipped his head and gave Edward a stare that remained level while the rest of him wobbled around it.

"Weedy," piped up Carlton. "Don't worry yourself, man. It's dealt with."

"Dealt with? Is it? Is anything ever dealt with where Prince Edward is concerned? He keeps finding ways to make trouble. May I refer you to the death of the Prince Consort, Albert in '61. I am only saying what we all know is true. The Queen thinks Prince Edward killed him, with the worry caused by all his youthful... shenanigans."

Boggo put everything he had into the word 'shenanigans', almost losing his footing. Rules staff rocked back on their heels, aghast 'ohs' knocked out of them.

Prince Edward stood in astonishment, his royalty turned to wretchedness. Of a sudden the jubilee bells of his personality, all those chimes of Bow and St Clements, which even with Carlton beside him had not been entirely stilled, now took on the desolate toll of a buoy rocking in the estuary, as wind gets up and darkness falls.

"You vile little man," he breathed, to the slow, rocking rhythm of that lonely vesper on a darkening sea. "As Rat and Mole Destroyer, you of all people should know it was the drains at Windsor Castle that killed my father, filthy as they were. But Her Majesty does not stoop to thinking about drains. She prefers to think in terms of personalities."

A Rules doorman took this as the signal to move forward and begin the rough business of ejection. Bruiser strength became apparent beneath elegant frock-coat.

"Leave him," shouted Carlton.

The doorman hesitated. Boggo did a slow circling, as though daring anyone to attack a royally appointed rodent catcher. He wobbled his attention back to Prince Edward.

"I have covered for you so far. All of us have. The latest embarrassment at Crystal Palace - turned it into a curiosity, a mere mechanical piano. Newspaper editors, hacks, writers, those types, paid off and persuaded that it was all a lot of nothing. But you would dare to risk that effort by arranging a concert at Hyde Park?"

"Weedy, it is dealt with," piped up Carlton a second time, though from an amused curl of lip, I had the impression he was enjoying this roasting of the Prince.

"Yes I have heard about your censure, Carlton, but I will have my say."

Boggo had obviously built himself up to this with drink and determination. Nothing was going to stop him, not even Edward's surrender.

"You intended to stage a concert in Hyde Park, where you could have been heard in Parliament, at Buckingham Palace itself. There would have been nowhere to conceal a new musical craze using electrical sound machines, which cause ordinary, sober British people to lose their sense. You would have provoked revolution, devastating the Queen, the monarchy, the country, with your... shenanigans." If anything, even more effort went into this 'shenanigans' than the last one. Boggo was left panting and exhausted. "You are not fit to be king."

Another 'oooh' from the crowd. What would be the Prince's answering remarks? The emptiness of a pause gave cause of concern. Was our prize-fighter beaten? He stared at the floor, before raising bruised eyes, as if grazed by bare knuckles.

"I know that for whatever reason your word carries weight at court. So be it. In these modern times we have to worry about plumbing as much as pageantry. No doubt that's all to the good. Better plumbing might have saved my father, it is true. It is also true the Queen blames me for his death. I know what it is to be a disappointment to a parent. We are alike, you and I, because you know what it feels like to be a disappointment as a parent."

There was a third communal 'ohh', suggesting that, in his turn, Edward had landed one. Boggo staggered as though a physical blow had indeed struck. Belle shook, and Maisie's arm went to her. I stationed on the other side, so that we could both stand with Belle in her time of trouble.

"Perhaps neither of us really deserves such judgement," continued Prince Edward. "But I tell you this, Weedy. You cannot judge me. You don't understand my life, or this music, or these sound machines. I am the heir. As such you could say I am the future. And this music is the future. You're not going to tell me what to do. There will be a concert in Hyde Park whether you and your people like it or not."

With these final words, Carlton's face, which had been slack with entitled self-assurance, abruptly tightened.

"Sorry, sir, what was that?"

"The Hyde Park gig is happening. I've changed my mind. If you don't like my decision you can get out."

"But we agreed..."

"Get out. Out I say."

The Rules doorman shimmered towards the table.

"Shall I have these gentleman removed now, Your Highness?"

"I am sure Mr Carlton has the good sense to leave of his own volition. You too, Weedy. Don't make a scene, there's good fellows."

Boggo turned towards the door, but momentum kept him revolving so that he ended up facing us again. This confused him. The doorman's left hand steadied Boggo, while his right indicated the door, which, after a slower turn, the rodent catcher weaved his way towards. I'm sure some of his disorientation was due not only to drink, but also to a breakdown in the organisation of his royal world. Royalty, after all, is a picture of order for us who live in a place where often there isn't much of it.

Now that structure had failed.

Carlton followed in Boggo's disturbed wake, his course clear and determined. I had the feeling he was going to create far more problems for us than Boggo.

"Right," declared Edward, his jubilee bells ringing out once again. "It looks as though I've come to my senses. Let's get Hyde Park organised."

CHAPTER 26

I found myself in Hyde Park standing on Rotten Row. Almanac once told me that this lovely avenue beside the Serpentine used to be called Royal Road. That was in the days of good King Charles, who travelled this way between London and Hampton Court. Just as King Charles travelled back and fore, wearing and changing the road surface, so words in long use become abraded into something different, even, by degrees, into the opposite of what they once were. That was how I came to be standing on Rotten Row. If I didn't know that Royal Rows could become Rotten Rows, or the other way round, I wouldn't have believed my life as it was now.

Prince Edward had been as good as his word. He now supposedly sat in majesty over preparations for a concert that would burst us into the world's consciousness. In reality, he was distant from events at Kensington Palace. It was people like your humble narrator who were struggling to make things actually work. No one would listen to any word of caution. All prudence had been thrown over at Rules. I watched the jolly greetings and aimless carpentry of an operation that had none of the quiet competence of Mr Smith at Crystal Palace. Two grooms were discussing arrangements for parking the expected thousands of carriages.

"Look, we don't know where we are going to put them. We'll let it happen as an experiment. Where would we be without Faraday's experiments? We don't have regulation in this country, we have good, solid, British common sense. The owners of those carriages can be relied upon to do the right thing."

So it was that laziness and lack of foresight were dressed up as British virtues.

I looked towards the spot selected for our stage, at the bottom of a slope sweeping down from Rotten Row towards the Serpentine. Crystal Palace had seen us up on a terrace with a good gap between stage and audience.

"Is that the same stage we used at Crystal Palace?" I asked Eddie.

"Yes, what of it?"

"But it's too low. We were on the crown of a slope at Crystal Palace. Here we are at rock bottom. We need a taller stage to keep the audience off it. That thing is only about 40 inches high."

"We haven't got time to build a new stage. The longer we wait, the more chance Carlton and his pals have to derail us. So we're just going to put together the old stage and make the best of it."

"But the crowd's entire weight will bear down on a stage 40 inches high."

"It's alright. There's a plan for keeping people back."

"Oh yes, and what's that? I can't see the government allowing us to use the Metropolitans or the Army."

Fear had made me more forceful than usual. But if I was fearful up until now, Eddie's next casual remark put the very fear of God into me.

"We're going to use the Jovial Thirty Two."

Slack jawed, nauseated astonishment gripped your narrator as he tried to come to terms with this news.

"The Jovials? Are you off your little rocker? You can't have those people running security at a concert. This is going to be a complete fifteen puzzle."

"No doubt a clever boy like you looks down on organisations like the Jovials. Let me tell you, they have a coordination as complete as that of the Metropolitans, with captains and junior officers who impose order and demand loyalty. They will be well paid in drink, which is dependent on them not stepping beyond the bounds. When it comes down to it, they are business people like everyone else in London. All they'll do is keep people back from the stage. Who do you suggest in place of them? The nut and orange sellers? The flower girls?"

"Eddie, see sense. The Jovials are an organised, criminal mob. Having them here can only lead to disaster."

"This is doing what needs to be done. So we have to make a few, small compromises to help bring our new music to people."

"But everything could get out of hand. We have none of the support we had at Crystal Palace."

"We have the Prince."

"Yes but he's like an actor, playing a role. If you were playing a king in a play at the Wilton, that doesn't mean you can organise a kingdom, does it? It's all the people behind him that organise things, and they have been told to lie low."

Eddie halted his slow progress along Rotten Row, turning to fix on me a look that was all divine certainty. I would have preferred anger. How to deal with someone who thinks he is on a divine mission? When a higher power beyond human understanding has spoken to you, then human understanding, about bad concert planning or whatever else it might be, is not going to make an impression.

"You underestimate the Prince. He believes in us, and I believe in him."

"Believe all you like, it won't make him any better at organising a concert."

"This is happening, Tim. You were fretful in Chatham, you were panicking at Crystal Palace, but everything worked out."

"If I may remind you, we nearly didn't make it out of the

Good Companions. And at Crystal Palace, by a stroke of luck, we had professionals behind us. That's gone."

"Oh stop your noise. I don't want to hear any more about it. This is a new dawn. Everything's going to be fine."

CHAPTER 27

So with awful inevitability, Royal Road decayed towards Rotten Row. People were coming from all over. We knew that. Even though the Fleet Street news sheets on the establishment payroll ignored or denied what was happening, word of mouth spread despite them, the collision of blanket denial and wild exaggeration setting up cyclones of rumour, which no doubt caused more people to take the road to Hyde Park.

They were coming, and all we could do was prepare as best we could. The euphoria of Crystal Palace, combined with Prince Edward's impatience to demonstrate his opposition to uppity rat and mole destroyers, both conspired to push events headlong. The day after my walk along Rotten Row, I left my bedroom where I had been billeted, overlooking the formal gardens of Kensington Palace, and repaired to the ground-floor suite where Prince Edward and his cronies had set up a centre of operations. There I witnessed the chaos of organisation first hand. Royal advisors carried themselves with a Pall Mall clubman demeanour. If we could have had the club staff rather than the patrons we might have had a chance.

The main tool in use was, would you believe, one of Alexander Graham Bell's telephones. I watched the Prince speaking into a mouthpiece placed atop a mount reminiscent of a swan's neck, while what appeared to be a large playing piece from a chess set stuck itself against a royal ear. Apparently, the first person in Britain who saw this device was the Queen, during a demonstration at Osborne House. Now Prince Edward had one. I've no idea who he was talking to. You might look clever and modern with your telephone, but owning a telephone is a kind of achievement that means nothing unless other people achieve it too. Had the Prince found some people to talk to on the other end of the line, or was he just talking to himself?

"Try and keep them away from Kensington Palace," he was shouting, not quite able to get away from the habit of raising his voice in communicating with people at a distance. "That's where we have all our stewards. The entrances, yes. That might not be possible. No, we're not so much interested in financial gain. You have the money then, we will have the publicity. Yes. Keep me informed."

The time pre-concert and the concert itself merged into one another. Cap pulled down over my eyes, I left Kensington Palace, walked through Kensington Gardens, crossed West Carriage Drive, and stole into the rag tag host waiting for entertainment. The crowd was already heavy, pressing down the slope towards that ill-conceived stage. A juggler and a contortionist were currently doing their best.

The afternoon dragged on with drinking and carousing. I watched the Jovials who had an endless supply of free grog. When they were out and about in London, on their normal daily, or rather nightly operations, they tended to operate in small groups, to both minimise detection and limit damage if one party was rolled over. Now, at the centre of this vast crowd, with their full manpower deployed, without a crusher in sight, the Jovials in their top hats and black togs with silver accoutrements, were mikados. Nothing could touch them. This power, in tandem with drink, was going to their heads. People were starting to get whacked.

I struggled out through the main press, into a grassy area near West Carriage Drive where the first casualties of crush or fighting were receiving desultory medical treatment. This did not look good. How would we even get the band from the green room area of tents near Kensington Palace, to the stage?

Crossing West Carriage Drive, I made my way back along one of Kensington Garden's tree-bordered avenues, towards the green room tents set up near the Circular Pond. I could hear warm-up scales and practice chords, thrilling little vignettes of potential music. Outside the tent flap entrance, stood a man of short stature, wrapped around his Irish fiddling as a man on a cold evening might curl up around a hot cup of chocolate. He looked up from his music.

"How's it going down beyont?"

"Not well, Sean. The Jovials are beating people. Not even the musicians are safe. Just before I left to come back here, they whacked that bagpipe player from Edinburgh."

"Whacking you say? I'm no admirer of the bagpipes me-self. More a weapon of war than a musical instrument. But whacking of musicians? Is that what's going on here?"

"Looks that way, Sean."

"For me, I think Ireland is calling."

"I don't blame you, Sean."

The fiddler gathered his meagre belongings and trotted off in the direction of Paddington Station, his lilting gait making a Tipperary of London.

Inside the heavy military canvas of the tent, trills and thrills did not cease out of any respect for me. It was necessary to stand right in front of Eddie to gain his attention.

"Tim? You're not coming to me with a problem, are you?"

"It will take a miracle for us to even get to the stage."

"What do you mean?"

"It's getting benjo down there. The crowd is in a right mood after getting whacked by the Jovial Thirty Two. Why are they even called that? There's more than thirty two of them, and they are not at all jovial."

"Somehow makes them more scary, don't you think?"

called a gay Belle, not bothering to interrupt a sequence of ornate finger shapes on the fret board of her guitar.

"Tim, why are you always looking on the gloomy side?" moaned Eddie.

Grabbing my arm, he pulled me past piles of instrument cases, sparkly jackets and dresses hanging on racks, trays of fancy, half-eaten sandwiches, people sitting on garden chairs having face paint applied, finally propelling me through the rear tent flap. He gestured to a wide space in front of us.

"This is how we get in."

I beheld the black and green shapes of agricultural steam engines, smoking with intent, like a line of battleships getting up steam to demonstrate British sea power. Their crews were unmistakable Jovials, wearing tall, stovepipe hats, echoing the chimneys of their restless machines.

"Where did they get those?"

"The Prince arranged them, as transport around the site."

"When? I had no knowledge of this."

"There was you moaning that the Prince had no one to talk to on his telephone, when in fact the Lord Lieutenant of Kent is the proud owner of his own telephone. Last night, without leaving Kensington Palace, the Prince asked the Lord Lieutenant to call in favours with some local farmers. And here we are. It's the modern age, Tim."

"Do the Jovials even know how to drive them?"

"How hard can it be?"

I spent a nerve-stretching hour watching the Jovials messing about with agricultural machinery that should never have been placed in their charge. Then, as the sun fell behind Hyde Park trees, it was impossible to deny that show time was approaching. Everyone gathered outside the tents, waiting to board the ironclads. Belle had a full head of steam and was ready to go. The same was true of Eddie and Maisie. Tom was always ready for a gig, big, small, violent or peaceful. As for Whistle, he might have looked like a cornered rodent, but he knew there was no escape. It was clear there was no choice involved anymore, because if the band didn't play, he would lose the thing that ultimately gave him a freedom denied ordinary mortals.

In pairs, we each selected a mount and swung up onto the footplate with our Jovial driver.

"Let's go," yelled Belle.

With a blast of steam whistles, the traction engines lumbered forth, smoke billowing above the line of battle. We cleared the green room area, rumbled down a Kensington Gardens tree avenue, crossed West Carriage Drive, thence sailing onto a sea of people. Shouts of excitement, screams of terror accompanied banshee hooters. Individuals making noise all around us came together in one sound. It was that same sound as at Crystal Palace, a shapeless, primeval racket with all kinds of potentials.

We reached the stage and disembarked on a small storm-tossed, wooden island, climbing down with musical instrument-shaped luggage. The noise was a shrieking storm. Eddie beamed like a child who thinks storms are fun, because he had only ever seen them from behind windows on land, while a fire crackled in the hearth.

With evening shades dispersed by great lights shining in from latticework towers, he spoke into his microphone.

"Ohhh mama," he was saying, in this odd style of speech he had invented to talk to the audience between songs. "There's so many of you. Don't push around down the front there. Take it easy. Just keep still. Keep it together."

Keep still, that was a joke, I thought to myself from my place behind a tea-chest noise cabinet. The music about to erupt was not designed to keep people still. Music makes people move. Men singing while toting loads on ships; soldiers marching to the sound of drums and pipes; mothers crooning to their babies to aid a rhythmic rocking to sleep. Those are all orderly manners of movement, with productive work at their heart. The government would encourage that kind of thing. What we intended to do today, in Hyde Park, not a stone's throw from the British Parliament, was to play music that had no clear purpose, whether that was helping men work, soldiers march or babies sleep. Instead, our krooman music was about joyful movement for its own sake. There was only music and the good way it makes you feel. All the work had been taken away, leaving unalloyed freedom. Those people over there in the Palace of Westminster would not approve of such pointless liberation. Where would it lead?

It didn't take long to happen. My place of observation by the noise box was supposed to be in the stage wings, which is a term suggesting some measure of organisation to proceedings. But it didn't mean much to talk about audience, stage, backstage, stage wings. The whole of creation was just a formless mass of people, noise and light. As Smalt started to sound our Big Ben bell, the jerry-rigged frame of things began to disjoint.

Following three solemn booms, Belle played the opening riff. This caused the crowd to surge forward. Jovials leapt to their duty, enjoying the chance to present the nastiest of human instincts as the necessary keeping of order and morals. Sawn-off billiard cues flying in vicious arcs gave an anointing to various heads. Belle, focusing on her rolling riff, failed to register what was going on. Eddie had to tug at her lacy sleeve.

"Belle, Belle, cool it down. I'll try and do something."

The music stuttered and broke, as Eddie spoke into his microphone.

"Boys and girls," he implored.

He wasn't talking particular loud, but once electrified, Eddie's voice was the voice of God himself, making its appeal over the whole of Hyde Park.

"Come on," urged Eddie. "Come on now. That means all of

you. Let's just cool this down. Are we alright down the front? Anyone down there hurt?"

The turbulence settled into a kind of seething, as though sea and land were coming to some sort of accommodation once again.

"Alright. Are we there now? Alright. Something weird always happens when we start that song. Have we cooled down? Are we all ready?"

Amazed at Eddie's composure, I glanced around to see how everyone else was comporting. I knew Belle and Maisie had spines made of steel. Maisie in particular seemed to enjoy the fact that she could turn London into a frenzy with her delicate fingers on four strings. She acted as she'd done when I'd fallen off my bike, aware of what was going on but not too worried about it. Her self-possession in front of that monstrous crowd shook me. This girl just had too many strawberries in her jam for a boy like me. It was the same with Belle, but I had long known that, ever since I first met her at the Wilton. Caring as she was, there was a toughness with it, as is the case with a good navy surgeon.

Whistle, by contrast, was grey of visage. Aside from his guitar skill, Whistle had always been a bit of a dulbert. Nevertheless, it is easy to be brave when you don't really see danger. Whistle's appreciation of hazard and his steadfastness in the face of it, served to provoke my esteem. For such a man not to break took more resolve than anything you would find in the traditional brave heart. Long Tom, meanwhile, was patient in his seat waiting for the music to start again. It was all a job to him. He was neither brave nor a coward; he was a professional.

Once again, Big Ben began its steady, midnight boom; once again Belle's delicate fingers, waiting a few beats, started work on that rolling riff. She shared a mischievous grin with Maisie. Those two girls were something else. Whistle appeared to be in a state of advanced nausea, but there he was, chopping across Maisie's riff with his downward stepping phrase.

The band were about half way through Bells of Hell, scuffles breaking out here and there, patches of grass clearing and filling again. I could see the people right at the front casting glances behind. These people, a line of actual, identifiable human faces, seemed immune to the mass of hysteria going on beyond them. One girl looked up at the musicians with tears in her eyes, her hands flat on the stage edge, as if resting them on a kitchen table. She appeared resigned to her fate, which was not a good one. I had the feeling that she had come here with such high hopes.

Behind this tragic girl, the Jovials were a frenzy of violence, less gleeful and more desperate than it had been previously, like a proper gang fight rather than recreational activity. As Bells of Hell strutted and preened on its gothic course, the Jovials made an effort of all-out violence to push the crowd back. The crowd heaved away from the punishment, revealing an arc of crumpled grass. This glimpse of ruined Hyde Park turf took my mind to a tale Rawbone once told me, recounted many times, since it was a favourite. In his sailing days, he had once been on a tropic isle where one morning, without warning, the sea drew back, revealing oosy seabed, molluscs and fishes dotted about here and there. Curious onlookers headed down the beach to investigate. Some instinct stopped Rawbone following them, the feeling of an old Thames man, who knows that when a tide goes out, it will come back in again. At this point, across the table, in whatever hostelry he was doing his telling, Rawbone would lean towards his audience, to give drama to his point.

"You could only hear it at first," he would croak. "A roaring sound that's like the sky beginning to fall in about its edges. Then, far off at the horizon, it looks as though you can see that falling sky, in a long, white, crumbling line. That's when I shouted a warning to those who had gone to look at molluscs. None of them had shown interest in sea creatures before; why should they now? I could only yell once, because after that I was running for my life from an ocean coming back to take vengeance upon the land."

The crowd retreated into a crush that could not accept extra numbers. A violent return of the tide was inevitable. One of the captains, resplendent in black cloak and colour-matched neck ink, ran across the stage and spoke urgent words into Eddie's ear.

The Jovials now displayed that characteristic aspect of cowardly terror, which comes across the faces of bullies who find themselves in the path of something stronger than themselves. There was no way our Jovial guard was going to make a last stand. That might be the sort of thing that soldiers and sailors in Chatham would consider. But those of a military persuasion are lifted out of the real world, paid for doing nothing except fighting, never worried about where their next meal was coming from, frequently fighting an enemy they neither know nor hate. Their situation is completely unnatural. The Jovials lived in the real world, where people fought until they realised it wasn't a good idea to fight anymore. While a military captain might have demanded that his men fight on, his Jovial counterpart felt compelled to set a good example by taking a place right at the very forefront of chaotic retreat. That tidal wave which had crumpled the sky's edges was coming, and only the foolish would stand in front of such power.

Boggo had told me to look after Belle at Crystal Palace, but she was the one who pulled me behind one of the noise boxes, which acted like a breakwater.

"I tried to warn you," I yelled to Belle.

"I never thought something like this would happen."

"Eddie wouldn't listen to sense."

This was the first time I had seen Belle scared.

"You were right, Timmy dear. I always knew you were clever. We should've listened to you. Is this the end of us?"

Across the stage Eddie, Maisie and Whistle cowered behind another noise box. Through a turbulence of bodies, flickering like a Margate illusion, Eddie caught my eye. He was looking down at the stage beneath his feet, shoddy carpentry threatening to give way.

"I'm coming, young master."

I heard these words but did not know what they meant, until I saw the bulk of Smalt looming beside me. Formerly down amongst the cables connected to noise boxes, he was now at our side.

It was fortunate that the Jovials had run away. With nothing to stop its forward momentum, the crowd was now pushing through and over us. The same people who were the crush were trying to escape the crush by running down towards the Serpentine. Smalt pulled the noise boxes into a kind of fort and hustled us inside this sanctuary. It was here that we sheltered until a troop of Household Cavalry arrived and rescued us. I say rescued, but arrested might be a better description.

CHAPTER 28

I don't know if you can imagine the shadowy 'power behind the throne' talking to you. Imagine she's speaking in calm tones, suggestive of power in itself. There's no need for a raised voice, since opposition to her word is futile. Imagine glancing away from this hidden power to the heir to the throne. You catch a slant of him through a partly opened door, his heavy form standing alone with his back to a fire that isn't burning, drink in hand. There isn't much left in the glass, or in a decanter on the sideboard beside the window. The door closes.

"None of this happened. None of it. The record will be expunged. There was minor disorder here today related to noise made by faulty experimental machinery. Your equipment has been impounded and will be destroyed. Her Majesty's government is giving you one chance to get on with your lives, because a senior figure has vouched for your good character, and because your disappearance now would give rise to awkward questions later. Be aware that if any of you talk about what's happened, or recreate your music, then you will be arrested by the security services who will deal with you in the national interest."

I looked over at Eddie, a crumpled figure, all the puff gone out of him, his lightning streak face make-up now a party flare burning with pale flame in daylight after the night before. Maisie and Belle were not so much standing beside him as propping him up. All our musicians and technicians drooped around this central trio, no one giving any thought to resistance.

"You are free to go. Once leaving this building, disperse in different directions in groups of no more than two. And if you value your liberty you will walk away into a state of blissful amnesia."

Everyone hurried towards the door. Regulation groups of two began to form, the technicians and stagehands splitting off, Eddie and Maisie deciding they were a natural pair, Belle grabbing Whistle and dragging him out, Long Tom wandering away in the shadow of Smalt. This winnowing process left me on my own.

"Can I go and get my bicycle?" I asked of a severe gentleman, in what I hoped was a harmless way. "It's just parked round the back."

"No, that will be taken away."

"Probably just as well," I muttered to myself.

The lamplighters had clearly been called off in the area around Kensington Palace, which would explain the unusual darkness. I could see enough, however, to discern Eddie and Maisie disappearing together, towards Kensington. No doubt, they would find a safe berth. I hoped everyone might find sanctuary somewhere.

Dark shapes of mounted troops rode past the Circular Pond, destined to reinforce their fellows dispersing our audience. I could hear the shouts and screams of that business. Our audience would remember what they saw. They felt our music in their bones. But how many could write a compelling account? And how would those accounts compete with the government record? Almanac once gave me a book about the Battle of Culloden where the author laments that we will never know the number of Scottish fallen because it is victors who write the history and count the dead. The same applied here. The record would be made by others. By giving me that book, Almanac was trying to teach me the importance of writing. Without it, someone else always does the remembering.

Before I came to compose my own work, which now rests

in your hands, I pictured a narrator as an odd life form, which in profound proof of Charlie Darwin, has evolved abilities to see and hear everything. This creature would be part kestrel with sharp eyes, part rabbit with sharp ears, part mouse with abilities to squeeze into tight places, and part ghost, able to drift through walls. Using these varied attributes, the narrator would be able to visit all kinds of private corners, or fly freely from place to place, seeing and hearing events and conversations that would otherwise remain hidden. My own development fell short of such a creature - not having the ability to fly, or be in two places at once, or to somehow hear what is going on in a distant room. It's true that by some quirk of circumstance, the inside of palaces and business of kings had in small part been revealed to me, but there was so much I had not seen and could not do. A kestrel's ability to fly away did not allow me to escape over rooftops. Nor was it possible to disappear into the ground like a rabbit. Tim was only Tim and he had nowhere to go.

"Tim, it's over. I have come to take you back."

Did my mind play tricks, or was this some kind of spiritual reckoning? Such thoughts only clouded my head for a moment, before the voice calling to me settled into that of Rawbone.

"Tim. I've come for you."

Finally, the gossamer of protection, which had hovered over me in an odd combination of other people's wants, had gone. There was no house in Birdcage Walk, no park lodge in Beckenham, glassy accommodation at Crystal Palace, or lodging at Kensington Palace. There was nothing left.

The direction in which I now ran was determined by two things, seemingly at odds, joining forces to tell me where to go. A mopey, miserable part of myself thought there was no chance of escape. I might run from Rawbone now, but without protection from powerful friends and odd circumstances, Blue Anchor Yard would soon catch up with me. Old Ma knew people all over and under London. If capture was inevitable then it would be nice to go back and see the old places one more time. Yet even in running back to what I knew, a different part of your narrator reasoned thus - if they were chasing me, the last place they would think of looking would be Blue Anchor Yard. Both impulses were a push and a pull towards my old home.

I dodged away from Rawbone into chaotic shadows. I headed towards the worst of Hyde Park's chaos, figuring that Rawbone would not follow. This course led me back towards our stage, past its ruins, and thence onwards, hopefully to the far side of the park. All around was a ragged residue of our audience, easy meat for authorities seeking symbolic arrests. A couple of Jovials were making a run for it on one of those traction engines that brought us to the stage. On second thoughts, it doesn't make much sense to talk about running, when those enormous metal beasts only had it in them to lumber. While there is a lack of theatre in describing someone making 'an amble for it', such a description would be accurate. The fleeing Jovials were putting their faith in brute momentum and their position high above ground. I could see there was no warm welcome to be had on the footplate, but a precarious berth offered itself on a ladder leading up the boiler side. So there I clung, while the Jovials kept their pursuers at bay with natty black canes with silver tops. We crashed through park railings, which was the signal for your narrator to jump ship and fade into London's waiting streets.

That's the thing about London - you can have a riot going on in one place, while life elsewhere continues as if nothing is happening.

Since running might draw attention, I made myself stroll with the bearing of a London lad, who walks a road between law abiding as the government might see it, and law abiding as their own conscience and society might see it. This locomotion, a kind of watchful strut with your elbows out and your chin held high, carried me towards the river, its unerring line guiding me home to Blue Anchor Yard. I would hang around there for a few hours while they all looked for me elsewhere, then make a break on foot for Beckenham, which had looked such a nice place. There was a little money in my pocket, left over from my old life as a songwriter, enough to keep me going until I found a job out in the suburbs. This was my hope.

It felt peculiar to be running away and running home at the same time. I reached Rosemary Lane, where as everybody knows, Saturday night is market night. My cap pulled down over my features, I enjoyed the familiar scene. Rosemary Lane on a Saturday night is enough to persuade anyone to stop running for a while, no matter what the consequences. Hundreds of costers displayed their wares under red or white flaring illumination. Chestnut stalls glowed crimson with forge fire shining through the holes of baking stoves. At Ogden's Fish, layered yellow haddock glittered beneath candles stuck in a line of huge melons. The street blazed with an excitement of haddock, chestnuts, fruit, veg and meat, with people shouting:

"Eight a penny, superb pears, eight a penny."

I would say that just because something is a pear, doesn't mean it couldn't be its own kind of superb. I felt the anguished joy of living when you might not be doing so for a whole lot longer. That's the way to be if you want to see normal things as wondrous. Rosemary Lane was the place to feel like that, because there's no one better than a London costermonger at painting everyday things so you see them in their glory. I lost myself amongst all the people, hiding there until the early hours of Sunday when the crowd rolled away to its bed.

What I intended to do now was to use the witchy hours to make my way to London Bridge and walk out through Southwark to my new life in Beckenham. I was close to the bridge when Angus the Drop appeared, blocking my way. I saw in his belt the butt of an old duelling pistol. Firearms were not the usual way business is done. This wasn't Chatham.

"You were seen in the market, Tim. Do not run. Things will go much better for you if you just come quietly."

So, the decision. To run, or not to run? It's unfortunate that at crucial life and death junctures, you are less than likely to be thinking straight. If the tiger is coming for you, it might seem important to judge correctly about whether to go left, or right, or maybe up, if a tree is available. More important than left, right, or up, is the fact that you don't waste time prevaricating. The tiger is coming after all. So something else decides. Now looking back I felt generations of Tims before me, all coming together and comparing times of peril in their lives. They'd been long debating about what to do, so that they could give instant advice at this vital moment. Obviously, the two main choices were running or fighting. It was clear that all the gathered generations of Tims would dismiss the fighting option, because Tim had never been a big fella. So what about running? That was a much more likely course for us Tims. However, there was in this case a complication. The variously medieval, mud-hut, cave-dwelling, pre-firearms Tims no doubt were pressing for running, while those of a later vintage were advising that Angus was armed. Those of more recent experience counselled that there was no way to outrun a ball from a pistol. The committee came up with its considered view about what to do, which was communicated to me, who had the simple task of doing what they recommended. Now it's important to be honest in a book. Taking on the combined wisdom of historical Tims, I momentarily fainted. Next thing I knew, Angus's raggedy shoes were in my eye line, rough hands pulling me to my feet. Once back upright, those same hands obliged me to head down to the riverside.

"What's happening?" I demanded.

"I was just told to pick you up. Beyond that, I don't get involved."

Now if you live in the country, you might think all would be quiet and peaceful at this time of night. Not so the port of London, which never stops. A working day here lasts the full twenty four hours. And don't think the noise and bustle would protect me. Noise can cover things up better than silence.

As we walked through the never ending dock business, I did have some attention left over to notice the predicament of those poor souls working their nights away. I had turned down Almanac's suggestion of writing novels for the betterment of society. But coming back from the wonderful song-writing life I'd enjoyed, things looked different. It was hard on the docks. There was the fear of not finding work, balanced against the dangers and hardship of work when you did find it. Boggo was right when he said that a livelihood is misnamed when it kills those that do the work. Almanac once told me that averaged out, one man a week died in dock accidents. I didn't take much notice of that at the time, but now I had been away for a while, his words came back to me with the weight of their true meaning.

I reached the quayside, to see Rawbone sitting on an upturned barrel.

"Not the river, Rawbone," I wailed, losing any sense of composure. "I will pay you back by writing the worst kind of scandal sheet. It doesn't matter if it's puff to advertise bread that is mostly sawdust, I will write it all. I don't care, just let me live."

"Calm down, Tim. You ain't going to be writing no scandal sheets. That's not necessary."

"I'll work night and day."

"Calm down, Tim."

"I know I should take it like a man, but that just happens in stories."

At this point, Angus started laughing, taking heartless amusement in my predicament. Still, while he was laughing, I decided that maybe he wasn't concentrating on the job in hand. It was time to make a last break for Beckenham. So what if he shot me? It would be better than the river carrying me away into the night. Taking my opportunity, I squirmed out of Angus's grip and started to leg it.

"Stop, Tim," I heard yelled after me. This was the signal to run even harder. If only I could get to Beckenham. Belle might be there. Apart from parents, who are in a sense obligated in their duties, never had I been looked after by someone as I had by Belle. Even if a pistol shot caught up with me, she would make everything better with cloth and astringent. At that moment, with enemies all around, it was Belle who was in my thoughts.

I was now halfway across the span of London Bridge itself. If I could just get to Southwark on the far side, that would be outside Rawbone's manor, and the chase through someone else's streets couldn't help but be less confident.

Almanac once told me about a game he used to play at Rugby school, where he received his education. This game involved dashing with a ball across a field, while opponents tried to impede your progress by grabbing you around the legs. I thought of Almanac's schoolboy memories as I felt Angus's arms around my ankles, while the pavement surface of London Bridge came up to meet my face.

"Tim, stop it." This came from somewhere behind me. It was Rawbone's voice. "It's not what you think. Stop making a spectacle so I can talk to you. It was the right ring, Tim."

At least that's what I thought he said. It was hard to hear over the sound of struggling and wailing. I wasn't really in a frame of mind to listen dispassionately. I'm not proud in describing this.

"Tim, stop thrashing about and we'll talk. You needs to hear that it was the right ring after all."

Of a sudden my struggles ceased.

"What did you say?"

I sat up in the street dirt, just in time to see the approach of that same smart gentleman who, ages ago, said I should attend a ragged school in the Strand. He was now making a rush at Angus and Rawbone, his cane held at a belligerent, lofty angle.

"Unhand that young lad, I say. For shame, sir."

The swinging of the gentleman's cane displayed little expertise and less discernment. The attempted blows were arbitrary in their falling. For all that, there was much force behind them, deriving from two handed, circular swinging from the waist, alternating with an overhead pick-axe motion.

"Avast," Rawbone was yelling. It was difficult to work out if his imprecations were directed at the gentleman, or at Angus who for some reason was using his pistol as a club, or at me, as I tried to renew my efforts to escape.

My own calls to desist added to the cacophony.

"No, no. I think there's been a misunderstanding."

In the confusion I struggled free, and realised that London Bridge was open before me. Unfortunately, Angus chose this moment to hare away, leaving Rawbone alone to face the mad gentleman and his ill-aimed, vicious cane. Damnation. Freedom lay just across the bridge. Behind me, Rawbone was in peril. What should I do? My own desire was to flee to Beckenham, hoping that Rawbone could look after himself. After all, I still wasn't sure what he had said about the ring. But these doubts were beside the point. The know-it-all committee of past Tims, distilling their demands into present instincts, insisted I rush back to Rawbone's aid.

"Leave him alone."

That was the moment when an impact caught me around the head. It might have derived from the gentleman, or from Rawbone. It was difficult to register the details.

Now, more than ever, I wished for Belle and her caring touch. Through a fog I became aware of ministrations, of a sort.

"Belle?" I called with hope in my heart.

As the fog cleared a little, I did not see Belle. Instead, I beheld Alf, the one-legged Grapes barman. He was waving something under my nose. A deep-seated, burning discomfort announced recourse to salts. Noxious fumigation of my most profound sinus spaces aided return of consciousness, at the price of making consciousness seem a thing not to be desired.

"Enough, enough. I'm awake."

I came back to myself on a couch in Alf's quarters at The Grapes.

"You made that difficult, Tim," said Rawbone. "No more of the salts, Alf. Thank you for your assistance. If you would be so kind to get Mr Mayhew a drink, and assure him that Tim is in good hands."

"You mean the fine gentleman with the temper and the cane?"

"Yes, look after him. He don't mean harm and I've calmed him down. Now, leave us be, because I needs to talk to Tim."

Alf shuffled off, I hoped to prepare a little breakfast.

"The ring, Rawbone. What is it you were saying?"

"It was the right ring, Tim."

"The right ring? But it was Princess Victoria's ring."

"It was. But it was Princess Victoria who lost it, not the Queen."

"The Princess lost it? But Boggo said it was the Queen. If the Princess lost her ring, and I ordered the Princesses ring from Blackwell, then that means…"

"Yes, Tim?"

"That means the wrong ring I had made was actually the right ring after all."

"Praise be. He gets it."

"But Angus had a pistol."

"Sorry about that. It was unable to fire anything. He merely carries it for effect."

I tried to take in this change of fortune. Once again the tide had turned, as it does over the mud flats, giving a body little time to adapt.

"So I'm alright?"

"You is."

"Well I would just like to register a complaint about the royals and their names. Their confusing nature is a national disgrace."

Rawbone nodded in the way parents have, when their children say that they have come home from a day of riding dragons.

"I've been shaken to bits by this whole thing, Rawbone."

"I understand that, Tim. You weren't the only one to become muddled by all those women named Victoria. It transpires that Boggo's sources were similarly confused, what with trying not to mention a privy and anyone royal in the same sentence. Boggo was found in possession of Princess Victoria's ring, which did not go well for him. His protestations of innocent misapprehension were dismissed. I believe he might escape prison, but he has been kicked out of Buckingham Palace and lost his place at the Metropolitan Board of Works. Forbes told us the whole story. He arranged it so we got the reward. Old Ma is in a right cheery gaudeamus about the whole thing."

It was Boggo who was in my thoughts just at that moment. A royal retainer, announcing that Prince Edward was not fit to be king, in a place of public refreshment, might as well have walked straight to the river and thrown himself in. They would have found a way to get rid of him, no matter what. If it hadn't been the ring, it would have been something else - a rat released in the Queen's quarters and the blame of it falling on Boggo. One way or another he didn't stand a chance.

"I feel sorry for Boggo. He isn't all bad."

"It is helpful for us that he has gone."

"Rawbone, I tell you in all honesty, it probably won't make

much difference. Anyone can see what they are doing down on the Embankment. They're taking London apart above and below. The future's coming whether we like it or not."

"That may be true, but it would not be right for us to assist the future in sweeping us away. Boggo was out to destroy our way of life. You are always too ready to see the best in people."

"Well if I did, that was an especial thing I learnt from you."

Rawbone studied me, as if I was one of his most needful vulnerables.

"I am sorry for all your trouble, Tim, but we couldn't find you to tell you to come back in. Let's look on the bright side. I think overall it's done you good to get out and see the world."

My body felt empty with relief, as though the worry draining away had taken everything else about me with it.

It was at this point that Rawbone reached into a pocket within his pearl seams waistcoat, and pulled out a roll of bills.

"This is for you. It's your cut - of the reward and proceeds of the sale of the real ring, which we did find and sold overseas."

I looked at the wealth that had been placed in my hand, and saw that working would not be necessary for a good while.

"Thank you, Rawbone."

"Put it away then, lad. It's not good to leave monkeys like that lying around."

I did as told.

I took the tankard of stout Rawbone had placed on the table for me, and wondered how I was going to avoid that amount of vile, dark liquid without hurting anyone's feelings.

"Where's Almanac, Rawbone?" I asked on a chance, reminded of him by the drink.

"He passed away, Tim. The typhoid got him."

I digested this for a moment. He was my teacher. Now with an empty feeling collapsing the already empty sack of my insides, I realised it was just me trying to work out what to do.

"That's sad news, Rawbone."

"Ay that it is. But he had a good life with us, who accepted him for what he was. Some of the monkeys in your pocket is from him. He left it to you in his will."

I dipped my head at this news, and knew I had to change the subject or become prey to emotion, which is not usually welcomed unless it derives from some melodrama playing at a penny gaff. If you are going to have emotion in London, then it has to be so big that you don't have to take it seriously. Other more real outward forms of feeling generally have to be left alone.

"I don't know what to do, Rawbone."

"This is what you should do. I have heard tell that you experienced all kinds of future things that our grimy present can only dream of. Write up what happened, and put it in a safe place. I know it's impossible to say anything now, but one day life could be different. One day there might be need of a book as describes what you did."

I thought for a long moment about what Rawbone said. He was right. Perhaps I was the only person who could make a record of what happened. I would go to Beckenham, find a room with a bed, desk and shelves for a small library. There I would write my own book. One day, far into the future, engines for making electric music will be everywhere, and dash my wig and trouser buttons, it'll be a measure of wonderful.

ACKNOWLEDGEMENT

Thank you to Sharon for all her hard work editing this book.

Cover art by Rachel Lawston.

BOOKS BY THIS AUTHOR

Secret Street

Rumours about Secret Street circulate the playground. For Paris, this place might as well be a wonderland down a rabbit hole. Her unsuccessful search does result, however, in an unexpected fascination with geology. This takes her on an adventure, where she hides her interest from friends, goes on a disastrous pony trek, apparently saves the Earth from meteorites, and faces a clifftop crisis, which puts her in great danger. Through all this, she begins to understand the epic stories to be found in the rocks beneath her feet, whilst also uncovering a few hidden secrets in her own life.

Best Eight

The King of Earth - nominated long ago because of his experience as monarch of a small island in northern Europe - faces the end of his reign. There is the tough job ahead of extending the monarchy to Mars, which is going to be difficult, since Mars is hostile to Earth and its stuffy traditions. To prepare his young heir, the King decides to use the blunt instrument of university rowing. Why rowing? Because Martian settlers like a sport that demonstrates they have water on their planet; because discipline and effort are required; and because a crew is not simply a collection of the best rowers. Fortunately for a royal, a good crew is mysteriously greater than the sum of its parts. Even so, can a lazy prince, and quite possibly the worst rower at Oxford University, really be accepted in a boat? And if so, can he go on to become king of two planets?